Also by Dirk Wales

The Fall and Rise of Landon Harris

Shadow Angel

A Lucky Dog: Owney

Abandoned

Twice a Hero:
Polish American Heroes of the American Revolutionary War

The Further Adventures of A Lucky Dog

Love Scenes: Number One to Ten

Jack London's Dog

The Giraffe Who Walked to Paris

the last chapter is
missing

by Dirk Wales

The Last Chapter is MISSING

© 2016 Dirk Wales

ISBN: 978-1-61170-241-5

Cover design and interior layout by Lucy Morrison

Published by:

 **Robertson Publishing**™
Fremont, California USA
www.RobertsonPublishing.com

Printed in the USA and UK on acid-free paper.
To purchase additional prints of this book go to:

   amazon.com

   barnesandnoble.com

Table of Contents

Prologue

Prologue

"Dammit, I like this book, no matter how it ends... yes, I know we have to find "the real ending" — someone should write a novel about a novelist who disappears a few pages and a whole chapter before the work is finished."

Jonas Keppleman looked up to the small table of two people watching him and smiled. They were looking at him as if he were some sort of a science fiction apperition rather than the Editor of a mainstream publishing company with Sixth Avenue in New York right out the window behind him. Janet smiled,she liked his sense of the absurd in the midst of a lot of folks who didn't seem real or to have a sense of humor. But, she didn't say anything.

"More to the point, Jonas, we need to get the missing six pages of Chapter 14 and the whole of Chapter 15 — I need not tell you that deadline is only 32-33 days away."

Keppleman smiled at Alex Horn, who, if given the chance, would pull a knife out of his stiff suit jacket and plunge it into Jonas Keppleman's heart. This, Horn thought, would assure him the next step up the ladder and...

"All right..." Jonas seemed magically to be holding a key in front of them — where had that come from, Horn thought. Janet smiled at these goings-on. Whenever these two were put into the same room... well, what did it matter?   She smiled at her boss. "Let me guess, your extensive connections in Northern New Jersey stole that key which opens Joesph Kellnur's apartment door in Chicago?"

"How did you know... no, not about the key, but about my connections in Jersey?" Janet only smiled and looked down at her hands. Horn however snatched the key and handed it to Janet. "All right, enough of this… we want you to get to Chicago and find this guy's apartment, use this (and he held up the key) to get into Kellnur's place, open up his computer files and other stuff, find the missing pages and chapter, and FedEx them back to us."

He smiled at Janet and put his hand over hers. "Then, Janet, we'll send you a plane ticket to wherever you want to go and let you have a month to put together the outline for the novel we know you have buried in that thoughtful head of yours and bring it back to us for consideration."

Alex Horn smiled at Jonas and Janet as if he knew, positively knew, that this was always off to the side of their hearts, and deepest wishes, that Janet wanted to be the 734th woman to write The Great American Novel.

"Does it matter that this is absolutely against the law?"

"Yes, Janet," it was Jonas now, "it matters and No, it doesn't matter, we have 33 days to get this on press for the Advance copies needed and we have, in hand, what we know will be a winning piece of fiction. We expect no Pulizer Prizes, all we want to do is make back our advance and have a good book in the next line up."

Both the men looked at Janet Kidder. She in turn looked at each one of them and nodded at them, these two driven men.

"Fine… I'll be in touch."

DAY ONE

The Poems

She jiggled the key in the lock, not understanding why the door did not open for her. Finally, she looked closely at the key to see she had tried to fit it in upside down. She shook her head at herself, turned the key over and easily opened the door. After a few steps, she said to herself, well, now I am inside the apartment of this writer man whom everyone is wondering where he is, why he has gone missing, and most of all, can I, the newest literary detective in Chicago, find the needed Last Chapter of The Book To Be Published. After all, the book is 33 days to deadline and we are only missing the last chapter and a few pages… how difficult could that be?

Janet smiled to herself. She had never seen such concern in an Editorial Department. Because of this they thought it best to steal a key and assign her to go, stand in the middle of Joseph Kellnur's apartment in Chicago to see if the final pages might be laying around the apartment of their promising novelist. And, now here she was…

She looked for a place to sit and settle and — just look. The first thing she noticed about Kellnur's apartment, was that she was sitting on the end of the bed, which was not in the bed-room, but was in the living room of the apartment. The bed was surrounded by piles and stacks of papers, some in neatly formed mini-stacks and some in high disarray. There was a desk across from the bed, there was no televsion set, there was artwork clinging to every available space on the walls — she looked up for a moment to see if there was any on the ceiling — and then smiled at her own joke. Janet's first insight as assistant Editor and Interloper was that this would be one of the most unique assignments of her life. She was thankful that she had recently read Kellnur's last novel, **The Dark Room**, had thought it a good read. Beyond that, she also wondered if her bosses had done their proper homework and that Joseph Kellnur had indeed disappeared, "gone missing" in their terminology, or if she would be in the middle of one of the seeming hundreds of stacks of paper edging the floor in this misguided bedroom, and she would hear a crisp sound of a key right side up being turned in the lock and Joe Kellnur would walk into his own apartment and demand to know what in the world she was doing here, and – who – was – she?!

OhmyGod… she thought, there was nothing in her sedate life to prepare her for that kind of a surprise. She looked around in this livingbedroom with its large piles of paper and its organized disarray. Janet Kidder sat for a good half hour just looking, sensing and feeling herself in this space.

The good thing was that Janet, an admittedly compulsive, maybe even an over-organized person — when she walked into a project, idea or place, she liked to graze at the beginning. That is, look around casually, as if a sightseer or visitor. Get the feel of the place, and in her own way, to see if the space had an idea or sense of itself.

She had been given a stolen key and had admitted herself into his space… obviously, again, against the law. She tried not to think about that. She had come through the door on the first floor which led to a stairway with a stair landing as one might find at a library: seating arrangements and a bookcase with a full array of miscellaneous titles, then another stairway leading to his front door and the apartment.

Now she was in the main room of the large apartment. On her left was a large bay window facing the front yard of the building and the street. To her right was a large wall of windows facing a river. What river? she thought, as she looked down on it in the back yard. Oh, yes, it must be a branch of the Chicago River… she had seen this on arrival but was unfamiliar with the inner working/flowing of this river.

She was in the middle of this space, not the living room, but now the bedroom-working-thinking space. Behind the bed was a mantle and a faux fireplace. Arrayed around this, the space of a working writer… a desk with a computer and handwriting place and then many book cases and piles and piles of paper. Very strange, who would do this? And, a second thought, should she be nervous about this, I mean… well, yes, fine, this is a wrong thing to do, but here I am.

Not to be distracted. Let's do some serious grazing in preparation for… well, not certain what will develop.

Janet leafed through piles of paper, idly, as if they didn't matter. There were piles of paper, colorful folders and stacks of books everywhere. But, if she wanted to "get an idea," she had to prepare herself for the firestorm she suspected lay ahead, as well as the huge surprises… and here was one in the sixth pile of papers, stacked on the side of a small desk.

This file had a sheaf of poems. Whose, she thought? Kellnur didn't write poetry. In all the material she had read as background for this assignment, there was no hint of "poems," yet here they were. She stopped grazing immediately… clearing a space to sit again on the end of the bed and read carefully through the single sheets.

She loved the poem titles:

The Sun, the Moon and the Stars

In the Garden of the Hummingbirds

The Body Bakery

Surrender

White Feather

The Storm

Soft Night Train

(and a poem by John Ashbury)

She read the first poem…

The Sun, the Moon and the Stars

There was a time when the sun and the moon
were together.
A perfect union reflecting oneness in the universe.
One day, for there was no night,
Moon went out and discovered stars.
"Look," he said to Sun,
"how beautiful are the stars."

Sun had never had anyone but Moon
look upon her,
nor had she had to share moon with any other element.
She turned her bright gaze on the stars
and melted them away.

Moon was sad. He had never had friends like the stars before.
Moon went to Sun and asked her if she was jealous
of the stars,
if she thought the stars could ever take her place.

Sun looked deeply into moon.
He was the only element in the universe who could
withstand her intensity.
He did not waver.

"Yes," she said, "I am jealous of the stars."
Moon watched her lovingly.
"Mine is the brightest light in the universe.
You have never needed others before.
Am I not still the center of your universe?"

"Yes," said Moon, "but are not the stars very beautiful?"

"I am beautiful, you have said so yourself."

"Yes, but could we not share the vast sky with the stars?"

"I wish there was a place I could go to be
without these thoughts of losing you and gaining the meddlesome stars."

The moon nodded
and created night for the stars and day for the sun
so she would be forever happy,
and they would meet twice each day.

Janet looked up and around her as if someone had spoken. But, she was alone. Without thinking, she turned to the next poem...

The Soft Night Train

A freight train made of pillows rushes through the night.

Wind whistles through the ticking, the stripes whirl in the darkness.

Thus, a force of love is brought to the sleepyheads in the countryside.

Hard love becomes soft, overnight.

Wished-for-love is delivered as freight.

The conductor conducts this overture as he might
Debussy or Strauss.

The moon sets, the sun rises, the train disappears.

The pillowed freight train does not operate in daylight.

What an image, she thought, and how lovely is the flow of the piece… and she felt herself relaxing as…

        …her hand leafed to the next poem…

Surrender

Surrender is not giving in.
Surrender is letting go.

Surrender is not domination.
Surrender is freedom.

Surrender is not under,
it's over.

Surrender is not the end.
Surrender is the beginning.

Surrender is good,
not evil,
not military,
not captured,
but released.

How can I convince you to
Surrender?

"What's going on here?" Janet said out loud, and then looked around to see who she might be talking to. She was still alone. Joe Kellnur is a good writer, the last novel and the promising pages of the new one said so, but these poems were quite evocative. What has she discovered here? — and then a quiet moment, should she tell anyone else about this? Not sure... but, it certainly felt good to her. Yes, indeed...

... she was surprised to look and see that at the bottom of each poem Kellnur had noted his initials,

J K

…and these initials were the same as hers: J K, Janet Kidder. "… how odd…" but caught the thought in mid-air: Well, yes, it's a coincidence, isn't it? No matter, she thought. But then, Janet Kidder wasn't sure that's what she really felt.

Her eyes fell to the next poem… but there was handwriting on the top of the page…

"this one by Ashbury… marvelous…"

Somewhere someone is traveling furiously toward you,

at incredible speed, traveling day and night,

through blizzards and desert heat,

across torrents, through narrow passes.

But will he know where to find you,

Recognize you when he sees you,

Give you the thing that he has for you?

Janet sat on the edge of Kellnur's bed and felt something she almost never felt… dumbstruck… how could this man who had written **The Dark Room,** this multi-faceted, sexy novel that had given him a name as a promising author — how could he have written these? Not only that, but each poem was different in style and thought, as if written by different people!

Then, a second thought. I *am* worried about what might happen if he walked in this minute and surprised me, but maybe it would be OK, and it won't hurt to keep an eye and ear on the front door.

…then the Ashbury piece. She had read John Ashbury, but not this special poem… which seemed to speak to her and what she was sent to do here. She lay back on the bed to see if she could catch her breath and her mind… and finally, where is all this going… I feel like I am tied to this freight train, no, a soft night train…

She wondered, as she closed her eyes, how many of these images would linger though this day and others… she had to get a hold on herself… she had to remember what, exactly what she was sent here to do. Right?

Janet was surprised to look at her watch and see that she had indeed fallen away… she had napped here for 28 minutes. Sitting up she looked again at the room, this subverted living-sleeping — and now she was looking right at the writing desk and the computer. She was torn between "looking around" and getting serious about finding what she needed and leaving… she continued to sense a certain danger. She nervously fingered the remaining poems from the stack, but decided that perhaps, for once in her life, she needed to attack the problem at hand, rather than the usual wandering perusal and note-taking. Let's see if we can find the heart of the matter.

She got up and sat at the writing desk and pushed the spacer key to find that the computer was on! How could that be… no turn on, no password, nothing but the easy ability to see if she could find the files. This was absurd! She fumbled though the files and found all the usual suspects… correspondence (would she regret doing this?), the book files from the earlier novel she had read… seeming hudreds of random files, but then…there it was, the novel in question:

The Inn of Storms.

She pulled up the **Inn of Storms** files and found what was called **The Book Itself**… cute, Mr. Kellnur. She seemed to have the main file… but as she scrolled to the end, she found herself on the same page as the Editors… no ending pages of Chapter 14 and no Final Chapter. Darn!

What to do now? She closed her eyes again, as if back on the bed. Then, she looked through the computer files for poems… she typed in the titles of the poems she had read and found that none of them were in the computer. She reached back to the bed to retrieve the poems… she typed in the titles in the computer search and found no corresponding titles or an overall Poem Place.

That's strange. Is there another computer or writing instrument? Where?

She needed to read another poem, they seemed to calm her, but more than that, she needed a cup of coffee. The kitchen must be here somewhere.

It was quite orderly! All the utensils in a proper place. The counters wiped clean. The usual lineup of jars to hold flour, sugar, tea bags, all the usual suspects. She opened the drawers and found similar order with knives, forks,   spoons, etc, then, the messy drawer of larger kitchen tools, a drawer of cloth napkins, a drawer of paper napkins, a drawer of this and a drawer of that.

How, Janet wondered, could it be that the rest of Kellnur's place felt like The Collected Archives of 371 Anthills and the kitchen looked like it belonged to Ms Average Housewife in some common suburb? Yet here she was in a strange kitchen making coffee. Well, fine.

It was clear now to Janet that she was going to have to keep separate a part of herself in trying to fathom the mind of Kellnur. So, as she made mental notes, the word "inconsistency" came to mind. She walked to the dining room window and smiled down to the yard and the river. That calmed her... she had not used the phrase "grounded" yet, but she felt certain it was coming. The backyard was to be her closely held "assistant" in this project. She could sit there and collect her mind, forget about the "notes."

The coffee was good. It helped. Composure was returning. Good. She looked at her watch, she'd been there almost a half day and there was no sound of a lock turning at the front door...fine, good... how about a calming poem to go with the coffee... this really helped.

In the Garden of the Hummingbirds

In the garden of the hummingbirds
flowers curve into horns and a muted call is heard,
while creamy sunlight filters through fluttering wings.

In the garden of the hummingbirds soft concerts
melt the mind into evening silence.
Moonlight creates flowing star clusters in the shadows.

In the garden of the hummingbirds
the world folds into fragile peace
as creatures make pillows in midair.

Oh my, yes, that certainly helps... nothing like a cup of coffee and a soft poem to relieve anxiety... so, let's move on here, Soldier!

Janet spent the remainder of that first day, from coffee in the mid-morning, to 4:11 that afternoon exploring this man's life as curated in this large living-bedroom, multi-faceted apartment. Fortunately, she was a hopeless note taker. No telling what these could be used for later — huh, later. Well, yes, Janet, she said to herself, there will be a later, you-will-find-something-here. Keep at it.

Thankfully, she found no more stacks of poems on that first day... she had carefully put the file of poems in her briefcase, with a note to remind her to make a copy of them and put them back where she found them. But there were more and more distractions, and many more piles and stacks of papers containing endless attractions. It was clear that her briefcase would be bulging as she left, but...

...it was later than she expected on this first day... hmm...this first day, but then it-was-time-to-call-it-a-day...

...away...

...but, without "the pages"

Darn, again.

DAY TWO
The Table Room

Janet was surprised to turn the key right side up and open the door to Kellnur's apartment and not feel like she was "starting over…"

But, it wasn't to be that way on this day… she was immediately caught in the same net she had been in yesterday… this place defied any reasonable description of "…a person's apartment" …yet here she was again… caught again.

…it was the walls that might have caught her attention at first had she not stumbled on the file of poems. She was not used to "distraction" and wondered if she was not at The Center for Distraction North. The walls were filled with framed and unframed artwork. No paintings, but collage, assemblage, a couple of Polish posters for cinema, boxes of art *à la* Joseph Cornell or others who followed his lead. Plus, of course, the usual framed prints of a variety of artists. In a certain sense, Janet thought, there is a "gallery of art" feeling here. She loved that!

But, looking further, that sense was hit by a jarring section of notes taped to the wall. There were newspaper clippings and images, an occasional theater program, plus an endless array of reminder notes to himself. In a way, this section of the living room wall was its own artistic collage. Janet paused, this gets stranger and stranger… after all, she was only looking into the place of a writer with a bit of presence who had disappeared. She continually forced herself not to consider where or why Joseph Kellnur may have disappeared. She was here to look for something specific — pages for the Editors, and she had convinced herself that the discovery of the file of poems would repeat itself in the form of the end of the needed novel, or notes to lead the way to that ending. She realized that she was at the center of a life that was obviously full and waywardly mysterious, even though that life was not present here yet... yet? Would she hear a key-at-the-door?

Well, so what!

In mapping the place out, the immediate questions were resolved: the real bedrooms were used for other, more immediate needs. One bed-room was filled with personal clothing, shoes, all the necessities of getting dressed for a day. It had everything a second bedroom might have except a bed. The other bedroom was filled with tables, tables and tables, filled with papers and stories, as if that person was trying to organize himself concern-ing a number of projects. She had not realized, as she stood in the middle of this space and turned herself around and around that a writer might need, to *actually see what they were working on as a visible outline and direction.*

How fascinating. This table room was key and it might even be the key to how Kellnur's mind worked — maybe even a clue to where or how or why he had disappeared. Janet paused... looking into this room that seemed to hold the personal treasures that would become the source of his future writing. She dubbed this room, Table Room. She would be spending a great deal of time here.

Now, back to the living/bedroom mystery, she realized that it would certainly be attractive to a visiting companion — a woman who could be easily overwhelmed by the whole layout, forgive the pun, as well as the revelation of the man himself.

The man himself... hmmmm, well let's not try to get too far on the second day... it was clear that she might have to stop "counting the days"... this was certainly turning into a provocative assignment, a word that was not usually applied to what she did day by day.

She stood in the middle of the space and mused about the Life Commitment of Janet Kidder... could this be the corner where her life as an Assistant Editor took a sharp turn in a new direction? Should she be on the lookout for an unusual opportunity? This thought gave her pause... she reminded herself she was not a spontaneous person. Well, tomorrow is another day… and she hoped the beginnings of a plan of order. She looked around again… this did not look like a place where Order Made Sense.

And yet, "another sense" came to her. She was in a most challenging situation, place, assignment. Yes, she was concerned that Kellnur might turn HIS key in the door at any moment, yet, she was here, she was feeling and learning…who knew what she might lay hands on next. So, maybe all this was a, how do they say it… "a good learning experience?"

Or, was there a possibility of something else?

Could it be here on this outrageous assignment that Janet Kidder would happen upon another side of herself?

Maybe, not sure, but let's keep an eye out.

No One Plans to Be a Ghost

The next morning was light and bright. As she pulled up in front of Kellnur's building, she was reminded of the river in back… she already had in hand her coffee from this cool cafe she found in the neighborhood, why not try it out on the river side?

In back of the building was a most lovely yard, bordered by trees along the river… the river itself was good sized and flowing nicely. As she looked around, Janet couldn't understand why it had taken her so long to BE out here. A lovely, welcoming place. She found a chair and settled herself, her coffee and her mind. As she looked around, it was clear that if you didn't know you were in the third largest city in America, that you could be convinced you were somewhere in central Indiana… the peace was overwhelming. She would like to spend more time in this spot and, well, really think.

First of all, wouldn't it be nice to live in a place like this — Kellnur… she wondered if he came out here in the mornings to have his coffee and begin to think about the flow of words that day. If she was the writer she had planned to be, that is certainly what she would do. At the same time, she realized she was an outsider here… and she was at a nice edge of the north side of Chicago rather than the heart of the publishing industry in New York. And here was this lovely back yard for inspiration… already she was thinking about putting words down, one after another, day after day to create a body of thoughts, or, as she looked at the river… a flow of ideas, the beginnings of a story. Oh, how lovely that sounded.

…and maybe, once this was over, yes it would certainly be Over, then maybe she should find a "peaceful place" like this for herself, one where she could work — get it, Jannie, your-own-work.

Know what? she thought to herself... I'll bet I can get Kellnur's computer going upstairs and pull up a word document and write something. Yes, write something, didn't matter what, just set some words down to put under her pillow tonight to remind her dreams that she wanted to be a writer. Just that thought made her feel better... and the coffee was good... and the river was good...

Once upstairs though, Janet became again — instantly — the serious Editorial Assistant she was and began seriously to *search this messy place* for the wished-for pages... a chapter and a few pages. Yes, and she would tie a string about her finger to remember — HEY, JANNIE, remember to write down some things for YOURself. She started the search in the room that was Kellnur's organizing space... tables set around the walls of the room with files everywhere... the trick is: are they categorized in some understandable fashion? We'll see...

What appeared to be a line of short stories was right by the door:
(some good titles—)
Turn Left at the Smiling Cat
A Walk Along the River
The Song of Love: Tales from the 'Way North
The Invisible
Hmmm, *The Invisible*.

... here are the opening pages from *The Invisible*...

"When I was a child, I always wanted to be invisible. I made the mistake of telling my mother this. Stolid Dutch woman that she was, she shook me hard and made me repeat over and over that it was imperative to be down to earth... down to earth... down to ...

In reprisal, I did the unspeakable. I became invisible in the bedroom of my mother and my father in a series of nights to learn what only invisible children could know.

This was an important part of my early education.

Invisibility is most possible in this world. It requires enormous patience and the willingness to be frustrated constantly in the service of those few moments when one harvests "the secret." Secrets are everywhere to be gathered: harbored deep in hearts, kept loosely as change in the bottom of a pocketbook, or given openly in exchange for favors.

I have traded in secrets all of my life. They are the currency of the invisible."

Invisibility may have no limitations. In art, I remember vividly the painting by the Belgian painter, Magritte, who painted an embracing couple, yet both heads are separately covered with a cloth — a simple way to be "invisible" to your partner.

So, I intuit that there must be things in all our hearts and souls that pass the test of invisibility. The stories in this collection are that for me. These are ideas, things, places, relationships that I can see clearly what others may not, even in the stories. Like Magritte and all artists, we queue up in a parade that is centuries long, yet the eternal question may be, "can you feel something you cannot see?"

My answer must be Yes. I feel the presence, love and ideas of those people and animals no longer with me. I feel the force of my heroes... men and women who daily influence my intuition — the press of their invisibility propels me down the pathways of my creative life, a thing that itself is immediately and all-at-once invisible yet tangible. I can touch it.

And, we must remind ourselves that there are those who cannot see what is there in their sight: self-created invisibility."

What an insightful piece, Janet thought. I wonder where the remainder of this is? There must be more, yes, no? But, there was nothing under these pages and the next pile on this table was a short stack of small books with the title: **Impulsive Fiction**. She opened the top one to see that it was a Chapbook, those things that writers and semi-publishers put together for ... well, whatever. So, moving along the table she discovered that there were semi-corresponding, semi-orderly notes and odd pictures/ papers taped to the wall over the tables and their files.

Over the files called **The Inn of Storms** there was a map. It was difficult to determine where the map "was"...it was an island, a long one with a channel on one side, and an ocean on the other. Oh, of course, Vancouver Island, and at the bottom was the city of Victoria. That's familiar, then she noticed that a corner of land to the south and east of that place was the USA...

Oh, wait... This is where The Inn of Storms **is**... you are looking for pages that go in the novel of this title and you can't even see that this is *where the novel takes place.*

...his novel takes place on this island off the coast of Canada. Yes. However, beside this map was another map, torn away from its adjacent lands... but then right in the middle of this, it says "Ontario."

But, that's Canada, too...both maps. But why this map of Ontario with its city of Windsor with a big red circle drawn around it? Odd... but then, beside this map are two postcards... a picture of the Windsor Bridge, and another card from the Stratford Shakespeare Festival. Oh yes, I have heard of that, in fact, Janet recalled friends who had wanted her to go with them to this festival of the Bard's plays... but then, why is it here? Was Kellnur interested in Windsor? Or Shakespeare? Why? It's on the other side of Canada from where his novel is set! Do I need to start to "think" about who-is-Kellnur, along with the remainder of the assignment, recall that you are Looking For Pages. Keep moving, Janet, you are looking for pages and a Chapter... keep moving.

The next items on the tables were two sheets of paper by themselves with the title:

No One Plans to Be a Ghost...

Janet smiled. What's nice about Kellnur is that he does have a sense of humor and perhaps even an absurd one. Well, let's read *No One Plans to Be a Ghost...* She took up the two pages and sat to read and think through his new idea, and perhaps why he might be so interested in "ghost." Oh my God... what's next? Not only do I have to find "the pages," but I also have to get inside of Kellnur's mind, and do I want to do that?

"...but here I am. How interesting, I can't feel myself, there are no mirrors here so I can't see myself. But, I know I am a ghost. I can put my hands through things, I haven't tried yet to actually walk through walls and doors, but I will look for that possibility, sounds like fun. Hey! I never thought of that, Ghosts Can Have Fun? Well, I don't know, I just thought of that, but it wouldn't hurt to look for opportunities... ha-ha, people don't think of ghosts as being fun — no such thing as a Ghost Cocktail party... no trendy books about a ghost who meets a nice girl and they have a roll in the ether. Roll in the ether! Where is my mind going?

So, let's think of some useful (or fun) things that I can do in my new (after) life... perhaps even something useful. I am thinking back to the pluses and minuses of my life. What could I do if I was a ghost now that I couldn't do then.

How about a list of 'Ghost now stuff'...

A. Punish bad and rude drivers

B. Help the homeless ... maybe a series of 'safe houses' that people think are haunted, but I show the homeless people they are not, and therefore are safe and good for them.

C. Wonder if it's all right to try to get laid? There must be women ghosts, right? Maybe regress to a past life and find a girl I had known and come close with, and see if in this (after) life, she is willing. (But, if I can put my hand through doors and not touch the door itself, what happens when I am with this woman?) ...let's not wander off too far here, what are some other 'couldn't do's?'

D. What about 'telling it like it is?' There was no tunnel, no light at the end, it's just that suddenly you are — didn't think about that – where am I? — Good question.

E. I'll bet I could read minds, That might be useful... but then if I could read a mind, I might need to tell someone else what I read — a warning, a hope, a look at the future? Who knows how that could work out!

I think I am onto some thing here. Hey, this could be a whole new life — well, ha-ha, we don't know about Ghost Lives do we, except what we read in other people's bad books."

Janet was overwhelmed. What is this? What have I bargained for here? This mind, Joseph Kellnur's, seems to go in all directions at once. How am I supposed to respond to that? Here I am trying to do a reasonable and professional job, so Where Are The Pages?

She looked down to the next pile. What? Actually, there was a blank piece of colored paper taped to the wall over this very thin file of what, one, two, three, four, five, six pages... no title, no page numbers, nothing...

She began to read. And read... say, this feels familiar. She sat down and finished the six pages quickly and stared out the window to the river, which, like all of life, continued to flow and flow... what are these pages and why are they familiar and where do they belong?

As she read them again, she realized that there was a thread, the faintest one, that these might belong to the novel he was writing. They felt right, but, there was no way to tell unless she could match them with the existing novel pages, which were in the apartment that had been arranged for her — and which was not right around the corner, but down in Hyde Park at the other end of Chicago. She sighed a big sigh... but realized with growing excitement that if they were the pages, pages that belonged, she was getting somewhere. Then she looked around for more untitled piles or piles with notes taped over them that had clues or were signposts or… maybe the Last Chapter is right here, in front of my face. And as she looked furiously, she found… nothing. Darn!

…well, let's run back to where I am staying and see if these pages match the others. Oh, Lord of Novels, let it be…

Janet found her way to Lake Shore Drive and raced as fast as she dared toward the apartment in Hyde Park, the other side of Chicago. Even though she was racing in her car, she felt as if she was stock still, as if a freeze frame in a movie… if this was a book someone was reading, what would they think? Janet smiled and looked in the rear view mirror… imagine if the book gets done and some reviewer finds out about these six pages and how they got back into the book and — Janet came up against an imaginary wall in the middle of Lake Shore Drive: OK, these pages finish the next to Last Chapter. But, Janet Honey, you still have to find the Last Chapter… *the Last Chapter finishes the book.*

The movie metaphor continued in her mind, only now she was "skip-framing" up the stairs to the apartment to find herself in the middle of the apartment that had been arranged for her while she conducted her Editorial Detective work. Now, she moved to "skip-framing" thinking — What's going on here… if this were a book someone was reading, what would they think! This crazy, crazy story about a "lost writer" and the woman, who doesn't even know him, is sent to be the literary detective to "find" his missing fiction and get it to the book publishing people so that the book can be finished… hopefully a good book, and the fly leaf can say that "he lives along a great river in Chicago, one that inspires him, as his writing desk looks out on that flowing river." But, who will know about this outrageous story of the Assistant Editor who actually "found" the missing six pages and then was faced with "how to find the Final Chapter!"

…or, she thought, as the phrase "ghostwriter" drifted back into mind— what if she couldn't find, or it hadn't been written, That Final Chapter. Sounded like something out of a bad European book, well, hadn't she found a Kellnur piece about No one plans to be a Ghost? Well, don't think about that now… but, on the other hand, what if it hasn't been written yet, and then, who will write it?

"Hi, Jonas, it's Janet… well, seems that good fortune comes in small bites. I found five, ah, no, six pages that match the Chapter 14 we have. There is no evidence yet of a Chapter 15, but his place is like a confetti factory in a high wind… I am going to go back and dig even deeper to see if I can find the whole of Chapter 15 to bring back to you." Slight pause on the end of the phone, then, "Well, Janet, hope springs eternal… as it does with me, so, you are doing fine so far. Keep at it!

"Yes, I will… but be warned, I have no idea how long this might take… you have never seen so much piled paper in your life."

"Fine, Janet, fine… send us the six pages you have in your hand by FedEx for tomorrow morning and then, well, take your time, well, ah, within reason… and find the final chapter — remember you are in the city that produced Nelson Algren, Casey Whitman, Saul Bellow and now Joseph Kellnur… good luck and stay in touch…"

After a quiet half hour while Janet gazed at the colorful floral prints in the apartment after the quick phone conversation with New York — she wondered what might really be ahead of her. She went to the nearest stationary store to pack up a supply of notebooks and made a mental note to buy one of those cardboard/plastic cameras at the store in case she felt the need of a photograph or two, and then a wander off around the neighborhood to find a different kind of place for dinner and some rest before returning to the north side of Chicago, along the peaceful river.

DAY FOUR

Fav Books and My Sunlight Cat

As she walked into Kellnur's apartment and stood calmly facing his main room, she had a thought: I wonder if some evening, I should settle here with a take-out dinner, read something — there's a lot to select from, and then go to bed right here in Joseph Kellnur's own bed… she wondered what that might be like, what it might feel like to *wake up in that bed,* and finally, what might be the look on the face of Jonas Keppleman if he should find out she had done that! Even his New York sophistication might not bridge that.

Well, it's a thought.

Her second thought was should she take notes of her own progress and process as she moved through this assignment. Absolutely. Yet, her feelings at that moment facing Kellnur's life were blank. She remembered a moment from her own life when her mother found her crying in her room, covered with yarn, as she tried to unravel the ball of yarn from the small Christmas ornament she was trying to make for her grandmother. Her bed and self, that December morning, were covered with twisting and turning yarn. How to find the end of this ball of yarn, and then unravel it?

Janet decided to start simply. She walked into the kitchen to make some coffee, but, first could not resist looking at a row of books, quite neatly arranged on a side table:

> Two books by Anne Dillard:
> **How to Teach a Stone to Talk**
> **For the Time Being**
> A copy of James Thurber's **The Thirteen Clocks**

The Plays of Edward Albee
Sa Femme (a thin French novel)
Call of the Wild
A life: Vermeer, the painter
In the Lake of the Woods
three novels by Danielle Steele
The Life and Work of Edgar Cayce
The Uses of Enchantment
The Razor's Edge
The End of the Affair

Janet was stunned. Here was a listing of books, some heard of and some never heard of… but, Janet, you are with a publishing company in New York. If this man has found and read these books, shouldn't you also know about them… well, yes she had heard of and read Annie Dillard. Who hadn't read **How to Teach a Stone to Talk**, Maugham's **Razor's Edge** and seen Albee's plays. But she was stumped at **In the Lake of the Woods**, **Uses of Enchantment** (good title) and **The End of the Affair**. Well, here is a well read man. Fine.

But, before she drank her morning coffee, she stopped to make notes about **Sa Femme** and the others that she had not heard about. She saw her reflection in the windows that faced the river and smiled at herself… maybe there are some lessons for ME here… maybe I can not only find The Missing Chapter, but become a better read person who might some day write her… Oh, come on Janet, let's have some coffee. One last look out the window to the backyard…. she must remember to bring a sack lunch one day and eat out there. The contemplation would certainly be welcome, and certainly take one of these books out for a deep look… Well, first some coffee and then…

Beyond looking for "the chapter," it was clear now to Janet that she was going to have to keep separate a part of herself and her notes in trying to fathom the mind of Kellnur. She was unsure if this might help her think through the continuity of Kellnur's book that might go on from Chapter 14 to Chapter 15. So, in her notes, she made entries about "inconsistency." As she smiled down to the yard and the river, she noticed that calmed her… The backyard was already her closely held "assistant" in this project, some "peace and calmness" is really, really helpful here.

Well, on to a deeper examination of places in this space. Janet was almost afraid to walk again into the room with the organizing tables, but she did and she felt like she was walking into the mouth of the lion… well, lion tamers did it, why can't she? As she grazed the room, she had not noticed another orderly array of notes on the far wall. Must have been because they were more "orderly" …among them a short poem…

My Sunlight Cat

…sits and glows with the sun.
…flows with the sun as he moves from
sun patch to sun patch.
A warm and lovely life,
this glowing and flowing…and flowing,

… and then below this short piece, a handwritten notation:

" …what a treat to be with Samantha this morning… and the night wasn't bad either… but I was sitting on the edge of the bed and while her cat, a totally white one was lying on her back, paws curled and face swaying in the sunlight. The paws would wave lightly in the air above the furry face as her eyes gazed at me and I was completely taken…"

Janet walked to the window and looked out at the yard and river and wondered if this woman was Kellnur's girl friend and if it might be possible to find her? Could we assume, for instance, that Samantha lived in Chicago? Maybe… well, who knows about "maybe," then she looked down at the river and wondered if Kellnur wanted a cat, or better, why didn't he have a cat and why wasn't there a picture of Samantha anywhere here… or just some girlfriends or family?

Turning back to the present, she was faced with a colorful stack of… what are these? She leafed though the folders and saw quickly that they were a file of short stories. Of course, I should have looked for them right away… every writer has a stack or pile or file or whatever of short stories. She wondered for a moment if this was an indication of failed or uncompleted novel length ideas or notions. This of course brings up the whole notion of

How Does the Writer Think and Create?

Janet wondered how many lectures or meetings or coffee house klatches are devoted to the idea of How to Move the Story? Well, she had friends in New York who pondered these thoughts all the time, and now she bet that they all wanted to be standing in this room with her *this minute* to fondle these files and see what their final potential might be. For the thinnest slice of a moment, Janet Kidder was content with her life and what she was… the person who right now was learning the inner mind of a good writer… useful information for an Editor— and hopefully some time a real writer, too. Quite a comfort.

She walked into the bedroom and sat on the end of the bed and thumbed through the colorful file folders of short stories, this one has a good opening paragraph… I like the title… whoops, what does this mean? *Braille…* and it is listed as a "love story." Maybe it's time to learn what Kellnur thinks is a love story.

Fine. *Braille…*

The dog raced toward Todd wild-eyed. The barking seemed ferocious and it occurred to Todd that he might get hurt here. He looked around for a limb or stick... the beach had a great deal of debris. No, nothing to fend this animal off. As the dog approached Todd, he too became wary and stopped ten, twelve feet off, but continued barking, moving his paws back and forth in the sand. This was a lonely stretch of ocean, there were few houses, not a good place to have an altercation with a mean dog!

Suddenly the dog stopped barking. When he did, Todd had time to notice what a beautiful animal he was. A shepherd mix, he thought, with sharp ears and sculpted black and tan coat. Well cared for. This was no renegade dog.

The dog began to walk slowly toward Todd but would stop and look behind him, then approach a foot or two and then stop to look back again. Finally, the dog was within sniffing distance of Todd and reached out his muzzle and started to lightly bite Todd's hand. Quickly he pulled it back, but the dog whined and turned back to where he had come from. The dog wants me to follow him. That's it. Todd tentatively held out his hand to the dog. The teeth of the dog closed on his hand, gently now, and tugged at him.

They were both running down the beach toward the end of the small cove of beach. Todd couldn't understand the dog's di-rection...you couldn't get through or around this cove to the other side, you had to circle back and come at it from above. The dog ran around a large boulder and seemed, for an instant, to disappear. When Todd rounded the rock, he saw a dark opening in the face of the cove wall. The hole was big enough for the dog and large enough for him on hands and knees. The tide was out, so the sand was dry, but, a few yards in, it was pitch black — then a bend, then blinding light. He was at the edge of the next cove. The dog was sitting on the sand, waiting for Todd to emerge. This was a slender beach and around the point of it, a small house. In fact, it looked to Todd as a doll house might. The dog was racing toward it, barking and looking back to Todd, who by now had thrown care to the winds and was also running as though his life depended on it.

"Raleigh… that you, Raleigh?" It was a woman's voice. The dog barked and moved up the stairs and around the back of the doll house to the other side.

"Oh, you are a good dog. Did you find someone to…"

As Todd rounded the corner of the white clapboard house, he was confronted with a bewildering sight… a woman dressed in a bathrobe had put a foot through the decking on the front of the house, one leg was splayed on the deck with a slipper on its foot, the other was through to the hip into the deck. The railing was just out of reach, so there was no place for her to gain a handhold to pull herself out.

Todd came around her and grasped her under the arms and began, as gently as he could, to lift her straight up. "Does that hurt?" he asked, "Is your leg catching on the boards?"

"No, I can't feel anything, I think it's all right." Todd was watching as best he could, while the dog barked encouragement. "Oh, Raleigh, stop, please… we are getting the help we need."

"Ohhhh…" she said softly…

"…did you scrape something?" he said. She seemed clear of the deck because Todd sensed that she was as tall as she could be. He turned her body around and toward him. As he did, she caught her footing, and stood without assistance — but, her robe had pulled open and the tie around it slipped to the deck.

As Todd set her down, her torso was bare to him, her breasts shining in the morning light. As he looked down, he saw below her waist to a blond tangle of hair. In the sun, it seemed to also glow, both from without and within. He looked up to her face. She was smiling at him.

"Oh, thank you so very much. You have saved my day, and Raleigh's as well." She put her hand out to the dog, he licked it and whimpered. But, she seems not to notice that she is exposed. Todd turned away just as she stuck her hand out to shake his. Her hand met empty air as he stepped back and then turned again to her. She was a golden statue with an extended hand, her open robe as the white tunic of a mystical statue on a Greek island.

"My name is Aleta, Aleta Cameron." But, she wasn't looking at him. She was looking off to his right.

She is blind.

"You are very good to come to help a stranger. I hope Raleigh didn't scare you."

"Ah...no, no. Well, just for a moment. But, he is a good dog and well-trained. Uh, how long have you been blind?"

"Since birth."

"...oh, my God," he said. "Uh, let me... ah," and Todd picked up the tie to her robe and put it in her hand.

"Oh dear, I seem to have come undone. Sorry, sorry. I hope I haven't embarrassed you." Todd was struck dumb.

"Oh, I have," she swung her other hand out to find him. It touched his arm and she slid down to reach and grasp his hand. "Sorry again."

"...no, I mean, yes, you are very beautiful. Your body is golden. I, ah, I have never seen anything like it."

She blushed deeply. It was most becoming, Todd thought. Someone approaching them at a distance would see a woman in a morning robe and a man holding her hand. Yet they would seem as statues to decorate a tiny cottage along the ocean. It would appear surreal until the onlooker caught sight of the dog and its wagging tail... the only movement in the setting.

"Well, ah, what's your name?"

"Todd. Todd Ransome"

"I hope it won't be hard to be just friends after we have had such an intimate beginning. Or, would you feel better by taking off your own clothes for a moment, so you might be revealed to me?"

...she laughed again and didn't wait for him to speak further. She began pulling him along the deck before letting go of his hand and walking in the open French doors to the living room. Just outside the door, Todd stopped to look around the cottage, and up to the headland. He had lived near Laguna Beach all his life, but he had never been to this spot before. So much, he thought, for thinking how much you know the shore. This is the most isolated cove he had seen along the coast.

"Aren't you going to come in?"

"Yes, ah yes," he ducked his head slightly as he came into her home.***

As Janet finished the story, she felt her body go limp. She sat dazed for a moment looking around this strange room, and suddenly realized she was sitting on the end of a bed in a quiet room by herself. She fell back on the bed to continue her daze and reaction to this story of Kellnur's. My goodness, she thought, there was nothing of that in the novel he published. Of course there were sensuous passages and intimate actions, ideas and insinuations… but nothing like this… I just think I'll close my eyes for a moment.

And she did.

Janet woke up an hour later with that confusion a person feels when coming to in an unfamiliar place. She looked down at Kellnur's story, *Braille*…well, I'll never think the same thing about a blind person again. Maybe this should be a short day, she thought… We have a good start. Janet Kidder rushed out of Kellnur's apartment as if she was late for… what… well, just late…

She parked her car and walked across to the Coffee Clatch, down the street from her apartment near the University… watching the people she passed, getting her bearings, thinking about tomorrow… my God she would have to do this again… for days?… for weeks?… what could be next?

The coffee place had been an island of solitude. Mid-afternoon, there were few people and she could be at peace with herself and some really, really strong coffee.

Thinking about tomorrow — that she was looking for a Chapter not a sampling of short stories — or should she sample yet another short story to see if there was that same intensity? Or should she continue to work along, skimming the top of things trying to seek out the really meaningful. Or, or, or, Janet, have you taken a right turn here and detoured yourself too far off the path? She had kept some of the story files… she found a green file folder with a story called *A Man in a Cat Suit*.*** Well, how upsetting could that be? And, she caught herself… Janet Kidder faced in that small moment that she had, really had been upset in a visceral moment caught up in Kellnur's prose… was that just her, Janet Kidder, JK, caught up in a story of Kellnur's or just Kellnur himself? She wasn't certain what was going on here, but she read one more of the short stories…

A Man in a Cat Suit was a funny fantasy about an old guy, like all those old folks with a thing about their animals, in this case, the cats of this man and how he wanted to be like them, join them in cat-antics, so he got himself a cat suit and *became* one of them. Lovely! Funny! and now I feel a lot better… I don't have to be thinking *Braille*.

Janet finished her strong coffee and walked to her apartmement.

***Janet has created a **Briefcase Annex** so she can take home a selection of stories and poems. In this **Annex** you will also find the remainder of the *Braille* story and all of *Man in a Catsuit*.

DAY FIVE

Canadian Postcards and Stories

The next day, on the way to Kellnur's, Janet passed a University Library. She reflected on that and turned the car around and found a place to park. Up the steps to the front entrance and inside. What was nice about this Library was that it was old style, not modern, with lots of light and windows. It had high ceilings and a rounded top like a tower with windows where there was soft light. Around the main room were walls of books in the orderly manner of a great library.

Janet stood in the middle of this room with its high, imposing walls of books, and so formal. Finely organized as if a librarian could be a person who formed sculpture. Orderly, mindful, she liked that, it made her comfortable. As she closed her eyes for a moment, she "saw" Kellnur's place. The obverse of this.

Then, she opened her eyes to flood them with the orderly image of walls of carefully placed books. She closed her eyes again and this time conjured up an image of the dis-order of Kellnur's place and saw the difference between them. That must have been what she was trying to determine — order versus dis-order and perhaps where she fit into this and how to do something about it. Somehow she felt like she was still missing something, that she had not come to realize that... what? Maybe it was necessary now to look for a new path... idea... process that she was missing.

Once back in Kellnur's space, she determined it might be a good exercise to see if she could find out things about Kellnur beside trying to look inside his writing to find his soul. Would he have a soul? Certainly. So she set out searching the apartment for "things, telltale objects, tokens, amulets and what-ever." A way to "see" the man before he writes a word.

What seemed to be a common habit, was that Kellnur taped all sorts of momentos, notes, pictures, stamps and memorabilia to the walls in the various rooms. Janet started this quest in the bedroom that was essentially his clothes closet... there seemed nothing out of the ordinary in the closet and dresser drawers of clothes. However, here and there, the seeming habit of "things taped to the wall, by a mirror or near the doorway" came to notice. For instance, there were some Canadian postcards and stamps by the mirror. They all seemed to be organized around some sort of a collage letter/message in the middle of Kellnur's "overall collage."

The message seemed, on second glance, to be a collage of words to make up a letter from someone. The message was formed by cut out letters — the only idea that came to mind about this "message" was the kidnap letters one saw in poor old movies when the kidnappers sent hostage notes.

This message felt like that to Janet. So, in a myriad of words from newspapers, ads from magazines and other forms of printed words, she read...

Oh Joe

     how nice we are

          for us

               we live apart

yet share a heart

     (and there was a cut out heart)

     long   distance

       charges don't apply

come back soon

     to admire more   of me

          and I   of   you

    c   a   r l ee   n

It was a love letter.

Janet had to sit for a moment to catch her breath. How original and heartfelt was this "kidnap your heart" note. It must have been from this Canadian woman who sent all these postcards and stamps... but who is she and where does she live? Canada is a big country.

Janet began to turn over the postcards and notes taped to the wall beside the main note to see if she could find out more about this woman, Carleen. There were postcards of Niagara Falls and that area, and of the nearby town of Niagara-on-the-Lake, but also there were cards with moose or other wildlife, obviously from other parts of Canada... yet the main geographic area seemed to be eastern Ontario... some cards had writing... the messages were light and fun and intimate. The stamps were all commemorative and special rather than the ordinary postage people use. These cards and this woman were surely special.

She always signed her cards, Love, Carleen

So, who is Carleen? How did Kellnur hook up with a woman in Canada? What is her last name, and how do we find her?

Janet went to sit on the end of the bed and laughed out loud. What seemed most necessary at this moment was to begin a listing of all the mysteries. The Mysteries of Joseph Kellnur. What was that kid's book years ago... The Mysteries of Some Body. Well, she guessed, mysteries seem to propagate themselves... they need to, they must, they must... and my good fortune is that I get to solve this mystery. Lucky girl.

She felt that she needed to have some small encouragement... could she walk about this apartment and find something, learn a small but important detail that would give her some reassurance that there was hope for her and her mission and not a continual mystery.

Yes. But, what?

She went back to the small dressing – closet room and found something right in front of her eyes, she had missed this — laying right out in the open, on the dresser. A letter in the hand of Carleen and under it, a larger envelope. Yes. The letter had a return address to Carleen Bathhurst at a P.O. Box in Windsor, Ontario... I wonder where that is?

Opening the envelope which was still sealed she pulled out the letter.

Darling Joe,

An envelope will be coming from Northwoods Light with your story that won a prize with them... such a nice story, I am so glad and proud of your win here.

Hope you will read it to me the next time we are together.

Love, Carleen

Janet picked up the larger envelope that was indeed from *Northwoods Light* magazine and found a nice brochure inside listing of the winners of their recent Story Contest...

...and here was Joseph Kellnur's winning story.

She stopped and plopped down in a chair. She needed, wanted to finish this assignment, find the missing chapter, go back to her office on Sixth Avenue in New York and get what she hoped would be coming to her: an opportunity, the time to write something of her own. But, here she was, reading the work of this missing author — why wasn't HE here helping? Why doesn't he walk in — oh my God, what would he do to me if he actually DID walk in and find me sitting on his bed reading this story? Well, here it is, another lesson in the writing of JK...

Softly with Wolves

It was hard for her to remember... now, with him here curled beside her. First of all, she felt safe, something that had seemed... and... felt that it would never be again. But now, here in the fading mountain light with quiet surrounding her and him, it felt to her as if she had traveled to another world. Well, it was another world, she had gotten herself as far from that world as possible to this quietude. It felt like... what did it feel like?

She hugged him and fell asleep again.

The dreams were getting better now, less noise in her head, less nightly anxiety and more sense of... well, things are all right... safe... and him beside her. The war was falling away from her... the noise, the fear... fear that she would never again find peace... they certainly wouldn't find peace in that place, no one seemed to have ever lived in peace in that foreign place surrounded by words never understood, bullets and shell fire as common as birds in the sky... and she missed them, the birds of her home, far, far away, yet she seemed to still carry their songs in her head... in her dream she smiled and shook her head... and then she was awake, but here now, not there...

...but, he was gone... it even seemed like she remembered or felt him going off. He liked to do that early and she hadn't gotten used to it. She roused herself and pulled on a pair of pants and looked out of the hut. In one direction the mountains, in the other the soft plains, and she drifted off in that way to see if she could find him. She had gotten half way through the woods when she realized she had carried the rifle with her. She was trying to get over that... it was easier when she was loping along with Softie, it was easier to feel a real part of the wild when she was with him, though she was still trying to learn to keep up with him, he loped so fast. But then, he was a wolf and she was a girl — she laughed out loud. She wanted to be a girl again but it seemed to be a steep re-learning curve. But she was coming to the edge of the clearing, she could see the plains again and find him...

The shot jarred her, as if it had been fired in her direction. At first she ducked her head and then smiled at herself. No need to do that anymore and... ...wait, what's that! She looked through to the clearing and saw a man with a rifle. He was looking down and smiling... what was going on? And then she saw Softie at his feet and not moving. She watched the man bend down to see closer the wolf at his feet.

Ohhhhh... my God, he killed Softie, this rancher son-of-a-bitch. The man stood again and smiled, as if he had done something to be proud of... She pulled up the rifle and aimed at his heart and squeezed the trigger softly and easily, The man was stunned for a moment, then keeled over.

She walked into the clearing and stood looking at the man, now bleeding profusely from his chest. She threw herself on Softie, her loving wolf, and cried tears on his head. The rancher looked over at her as if he had seen a ghost...

"...whaaatttt...? It's only a damned wolf..."

"You killed my friend, you son of a bitch, and now you are going to hell for it... you aren't supposed to kill living things."

"...but you shot me..."

"Yes , not-to-forget that you shot him... and I hope you roast in hell

"It's only a wolf..." ...the words fell out of his mouth...

"...he was a better man than you... he gave love..."

The man had one more puzzled glance for her and fell away. She picked up the wolf and walked into the woods with him.

"Don't worry, Lovely, I'll keep you right outside the hut and we will always be together..." and then she had a thought. The rancher... they are going to find him and then come looking for someone... best to clear out of here... come on, we'll go together, just like I always thought we would... com'on, Sweetheart..."

She walked uphill into the deep woods carrying her wolf close to her... didn't matter what she left behind in the hut, she was going to start again. She had to...

It seemed as if she had walked, carried her friend from one end of Wyoming to the other... but finally, she noticed that she was higher on the mountain, far enough away from that bad incident that she might be able to find a place to go to ground and rest. She was determined to get her Softie to a safe place, to put him at peace in the ground. She found an enclave that seemed to shelter her and Softie, where she could rest for a day. She put him nearby and found some soft ground cover and settled, to be quiet and think. What she had not counted on was that she was so tired she nodded off to sleep with Softie's still softness touching her. A puffy cloud passing low overhead would see and understand that this poor wolf and woman had troubles...deadly troubles and that the woman in her distress had fallen away, overcome with her loss, the loss of her best friend, Softie.

Finally, she roused herself and looked around to remind her of where she really was. She was surprised to see a small gathering of wolves... three or four on the slight rise to her left... that would be the west. There was no movement only patient looking on their part. She quickly realized that this was most unnatural: a woman, a strange woman with a wolf, one of their kind, and they need not come closer to know that he was dead. So, the patient gazing continued.

Finally, she got up and shook herself awake. She patted Softie beside her as she arose. All of this was closely noted by the wolves... one of whom got up and walked slowly toward her. There was no menace, no growling, just slowly padding toward her. When he was close enough, he stopped to take in her scent. It had to be right for him because she was covered with the scent of Softie... oh, she liked that... the scent of Softie. Yes.

The wolf continued his soft, slow sniffing investigation. He put his nose closely to Softie... yes, he was dead, yes, the scent close to him was of the woman. The wolf turned to look at her in what might have been a puzzled way... what, he might have been asking, has happened here? He turned to his mates behind him and seemed to speak to them. They got up and walked slowly toward her and Softie. There was no threat, it seemed even like an invitation. Without words... why don't you come with us... yes, please. They formed a shy semi-circle around her as she picked Softie up and without even a thought, the group moved further west and slightly up the hill.

She was puzzled, but felt even safer than she had when she and Softie were settled below and off where they had come from – and yes, away from the rancher. Any thought of him tightened her body. Best not to think, just follow along with the wolves.

It wasn't long before they were up and around the rise, away from where she had settled. But they were in a most sheltered place. There were indentations in the rise beside them, the forest seemed to recede to shield them from the rest of the mountain and the land below... in fact one could not see "below," as if it had left this part of Wyoming. Suddenly, there were other wolves. Many wolves. As she was led into their open lair, she was surprised to see so many in one place, but there they were.

The four leading her nosed along to a dense place of trees, and then inside that density. She and her small party of four were joined by others who seemed to be watching closely, they all stopped and created a circle and howled... loud and long.

One of the new wolves came to her and nosed her over to a deep crevice in the ground... it seemed to have no bottom, yet she was nosed to its edge and she stopped as if waiting for instructions. One of the new wolves came to her and took hold of one of Softie's paws and tugged on it. In response, she knelt and let this wolf pull Softie away from her. Then another wolf came and took another of Softie's paws. The two of them, to her astonishment, pulled, in a very caring way, Softie's body to the edge of this crevice, and gently nudged it off and down. The other wolves then came around in a circle and pawed, and pushed leaves and ground cover and soft branches down and over Softie, as if to give him a proper burial, wolf-style.

Then more wolves came and as if it was deepest night and the fulsome moon had risen, they howled Softie away to his new resting place, along with, she assumed, other wolves who had passed over. Yes, passed over, in this peaceful place surrounded by friends, family. She looked down and said a silent prayer and sat on a log to see what would happen next. It was as if the entire pack had decided to visit her and wish Softie a loving-wolf-goodbye.

She cried. She had never seen or felt anything like this in her life. All was peace and all were safe. But, there was something else. As they all settled in this serene place, she was surrounded by their peace and safety. It seemed, finally, that she was now a wolf as well. That she had somehow, by some grace, found a home and a community here. That Softie, in his final mind, had given her over safely to his family to be cared for and loved.

This was Softie's farewell to his greatest friend. Now, she would be their greatest friend and they would see her safe.

Imagine, safe forever.

As Janet finished the story, staring at the pages in her lap… she thought, yes, what a "soft story" that is, goodness, here is this bona fide City Man who can write about The Wild as if he was born of wolves in Wyoming. Janet was beginning to wonder if anyone *really knew who was Joseph Kellnur?* But wait, right here is The Someone we can ask about Mr. Kellnur, if I can find her, and more important, can SHE help ME find Joseph Kellnur? As Janet looked down at the pages in her lap, she noticed that at the end of this story, there were more pages. More pages? But yes, there were two more pages with a note from this Carleen Lady.

The note said, "…well, silly me, I keep thinking that I, Me, is the only one in North America who Really Knows A Joseph Kellnur…nope and nope, you don't, Carleen, but Joe, these two 'story ideas' are… well, yes, different, but also fun and daring."

(and it was signed… Yes, and Love from your C.)

An Hour with Spanish The Inquisition

This will be spoken of as a very dense, thin book. A story told by a Jesuit priest during the glory days of the Spanish Inquisition. Beside the Inquisition Court, there will be four characters in this story:

Queen Isabella of Spain   The Priest, whose name is
                              Joseph
A boy child, aged 9, from Andalusia   The boy's father
                                           a dwarf

The members of the court will be variously described in their black cloaks and masks, as well as the texture of their robes and black rope sashes. The room in Madrid where this takes place will become a character in the story.

It has come to light that Joseph, a Priest, has questioned the existence of God.

That he has exceeded his authority in taking the confession of Queen Isabella. The insinuation is that they have been familiar, that her carpenters have made secret alterations to the Confessional of the Queen. That Holy Orders have been violated.

At the outset, it appears that this fellow, a good Jesuit, will be burned at the stake without questioning, testimony or other formal procedures. He is ready to die for Christ and he claims as much. The Queen hears of this and intercedes. The Court hesitates long enough for word of this trial to reach the village of Joseph's birth.

The father of Joseph is the most devout of men. His love for his son is immense.

He goes to a hut at the outskirts of the village and speaks with the dwarf that lives there. This dwarf and his woman, herself only a small person, not deformed, have a child, Juan, now 9 years old. The father of Joseph urges the dwarf, who has no name but Dwarf, to send the child to testify at the trial in Madrid. The dwarf agrees and harnesses his mules and he and the boy set off on the five day journey for the capitol city, Madrid, the heart of Spain.

The boy arrives as the trial has been turned toward Joseph's favor by Isabella, who insinuates that if Joseph is burned for sins that cannot be proved to satisfy her and the King, there will be consequences. No one has ever threatened the Chief Inquisitor before and he feels the need for hesitancy and caution. The other Inquisitors disagree and this becomes a conflict among them.

Finally, the child arrives from the village of Joseph. The Chief Inquisitor is informed that the child wishes to give special testimony. The Court is certain that this child will implicate the Priest and they will be able to sway Isabella from her position in favor of God, whom they represent.

The child comes to Court and appears to be surrounded with light. No one says anything about this simply because the Chief Inquisitor realizes that this whole trial is becoming something that could upset the force of the Holy Inquisition. The child testifies that it was Joseph who taught him about God, the holiness of Spirit, and that in the presence of the boy, Joseph created his father as a dwarf to show that God exists, and has given the Priest this power. At this point in the trial, the father of the boy appears as proof.

The Court does not believe. They ask Isabella to leave. They will now reveal Joseph's sentence. She refuses, as she realizes that the Inquisition intends to burn Joseph, the boy and the dwarf and be done with this.

Isabella stands and asks Joseph if he can turn the dwarf back into a normal man.

Yes, he can.

Do it now, commands the Queen, and the dwarf is transformed into a man, the light disappears from the boy, and Joseph becomes a glass of red wine on the table of the Court Inquisitors.

The Queen raises her hand and soldiers move into the Court to kill all the Holy Inquisitors.

The hand of God reaches into the pages of this book to turn the hour glass.

Janet stared at the pages in her lap, "Oh, my God"…and then quickly she looked about her… "…well, of course, I really mean, "Goodness, Me… right…" She remembered the Catholic kids she had gone to school with and how they were, somehow "different" than the other kids, with all their, well, just a bit different… aren't we all?

And then she saw the second page attached. What was this… more Crosses and Spilled Wine? Nope… what a marvelous title…

(Story Idea B)
[Some Complications in Growing Summer Tomatoes]

They met in the elevator, casually at first, but soon more animatedly. Each went to work at the same time each morning, so it didn't take long to find similar interests.

Unfortunately, their schedules didn't allow them to come up in the elevator at the same time at the end of the working days, but soon they found ingenious ways to be together without their respective spouses being aware. Yes, each was married.

Their building had a roof garden.

The man of the tryst had the notion of obtaining permission to grow a planter of tomatoes on the roof, near the sunning area. He was granted permission and the lady of the pair soon followed his lead with her own planting. They congratulated themselves on the wisdom of cultivating their gardens.

However, one night among the tomatoes, things got out of hand. They found themselves completely unclothed, making love on two chaise lounges lashed together with garden hose. Heavenly. The stars were out, the moon glistened on their wholesome bodies. All who have communed under the stars know of the specialness of this sort of union.

The tomatoes flourished with this heated attention.

The mechanics of their lives immediately became more complicated: meetings of the full compliment of two couples in the hall and elevator became painful, full of yearning and denial. Taking out the trash several times a night became bewildering. Walks in the Park became a lottery to see if the walk could be managed with the person each person really wanted to be with.

The trysts on the roof continue unabated. Tomatoes need tender loving care.

However, the roof came down one night late. The lovers had been together 'up there' as they came to say it with a toss of an eye. Each one seemed to need to cap off the evening with a goodnight kiss. So, each managed in his/her family to be the last to bed, to dwell on turning off the lights. They met, completely in the nude in the hall for that last kiss just before midnight. What they had not counted on was the summer breeze that blew both apartment doors closed at the same moment.

Each story, each piece I have found is different from the last, unique in its own way. That is the writer's accomplishment, each undertaking is its own and yet equally compelling.

Janet stared at the pages in her lap. Well, I have learned something today... I can feel good about it. And, more important, I have learned there is someone we can ask <u>about</u> Joseph Kellnur, if I can find her, and more important, can she help me <u>find</u> Joseph Kellnur? Plus, I can see easily that Mr. Kellnur, the author, is not without "range" as a writer. Each story and piece I have found is different from the last, unique in its own way. That is a writer's accomplishment, each undertaking is its own, unique and yet equally compelling, at least to Janet. The world doesn't know this yet, and perhaps I am the person who can reveal it to them.

I wonder how I can do that? And then, Janet fell away into a deep nap on Kellnur's bed. Like she was in a deep cave.

When she woke up, Janet was a bit disoriented until she realized, she was *again* sleeping in Kellnur's bed. Then she wondered if she was getting a bit more comfortable here than she should be. Well, what could happen if she didn't get caught by Kellnur himself? She was on assignment and it was certainly the most unusual of her short career as an Assistant Editor — and when she stopped to think about it, she had actually learned a great deal, which reminded her that if there had been this much, what should she call it, "discovery" in this-short-a-period, well, there was a great deal more to come. Yet, in the back of her head she had the sense that she was still missing something, something basic that would unravel this ball of yarn and create the final Chapter.

So, what was it, Janet? Time to go back to the basics?

Janet resolved that on the next day she would review Kellnur's one successful book, **The Dark Room**, and that she would do this in that fine backyard on the river. She thought she needed to remind herself of what Kellnur was at his best before she looked further behind the scenes, and there was a short stack of the already published book right beside his desk.

But as that next day arrived and she climbed the back steps up to the second floor and into the apartment, she had a change of heart from yesterday's thought. She had taped a sheet of paper over the door to the bedroom that had the tables of possible, fragmentary, maybe stories/books. It said, very simply, *Table Room*. It made her smile, as she walked into the Whirlwind-Table Room. As it had from the first, it filled her with wonder at the mind of the man she was — what, studying, trying to plumb, understand — suddenly she felt inadequate to that possibility. Her eyes fell on the line of pages of *The Inn of Storms*. Along the tops of the pages were a line of photographs of that place on the Canadian coastline.

Well, maybe it's time to go back and understand the thrust of the story, so let's go forward, let's take a trip to Tofino on the West Coast of Vancouver Island... to The Inn of Storms. Maybe, then just maybe she could determine where Kellnur was taking the story — what the last chapter might be like, if she would understand — deeply — the story thus far and then she would know — know what the last chapter should be. She had overwhelmed herself, not only was she trying to get inside the head of the author, but also, what might be the logical ending for the story itself. Oh, my...

She looked down at the line of pages marked Inn of Storms and taped to the first page were some scribbles:

(...in Kellnur's handwriting) *I want to write a novel of character and transformation. I wish to see if my skills are able to plumb the hearts and souls of four characters... two couples who go to an isolated place to celebrate — what — to celebrate an artist who has had a successful show on the other side of the world in New York? So the artist has an art-dealer... if the artist is to take his wife, then the art dealer must have a girlfriend... that shouldn't be too hard. (This was like reviewing the novel itself... good to be in the middle of the comfortable known idea for a change.) Could this art dealer in New York, smart, well-off, could he conjure up a "girlfriend" to take a trip with him to the other side of the world? Probably. The artist's wife had found an ad in a travel magazine about a place in Canada where you can stay at this lovely Inn and with some good luck, be there for one of their first-class-scare-your-pants-off ocean storms that come to rack the west coast of Vancouver Island. All right, then, let's celebrate at this Inn at the edge of the world, that is The Inn of Storms.*

Only problem is, says the scrawling handwriting, the art dealer has to find this girlfriend to be his companion. Well, he does that and they go with the artist and his wife — the dealer and the woman as a mismatched couple to celebrate the Art of Commerce — the Commerce of Art.

Inn of Storms, here we come...

and the end of Kellnur's notes.

Janet could see the smile on the face of Joseph Kellnur after he wrote that — this must be the smile that the writer lives for.

Janet's mind ran over the parts of the story that she had noticed from the book. The difference of character and outlook of the two couples... the conflicts that arise between the art dealer and "his artist"...these will be serious... the transformation of the woman, Hollis, as the story moves along... yes, let's remember that important part... and of course, the amazing discovery of what they call "Brain Island" — and how this island seems to each of them as a walk through their own brains... particularly inspiring to the artist. But she was getting 'way ahead of herself. Maybe now, Janet, is the time to think "grounded." All right.

Janet's fingers ran over pages along the line of the story until she found them arriving at the Inn of Storms... the two couples, Kerry, the artist and his wife. Hugh, the art dealer and his newly found girl friend, Hollis... here we go... though she had read these pages and knew them, they seemed to comfort her again — after all, these were the known pages back in her office in New York. How good to feel on solid ground for a moment... but, *where is this line of inquiry is going?*

Janet took the pages and slipped out the back door, down the steps to the back yard, and into a lovely deck chair, as if on a gracious ocean liner. She settled back and began her re-read of this chapter of Inn of Storms… why did it make her feel better… or is it, Janet, you always need to be on solid ground, yet you should realize that you are not going to get out of this without taking *the dive?*

She found the pages in the story where the art dealer and his new-found girlfriend are finally in their room at the Inn of Storms:

A silence dropped when the door closed on the room of Hugh and Hollis at the Inn of Storms.

It was a macro second, almost unnoticeable, except that Hollis felt it.

For a moment, she was in a room with a strange man. She looked at Hugh, but he was busy checking out the view, the bathroom, and finally, as if he had intended it to be of lesser importance, the bed. He looked at it with satisfaction, until his eye caught the sofa in the room, and he gave it an inadvertent pout.

Hollis noted this and proceeded to put her bag on the bed and take out all the new clothes that her sister and Hugh had seen that she had for this trip. She fussed with them, patted them, ruffled them as if to shake out the wrinkles. She hung them in the closet with elaborate care, with enough deliberation that it caught Hugh's attention. He slipped down into a chair by the window and watched her. It was good she was doing this small show, not for him of course, but so that he could catch her in a neutral pose. Hollis doing. Doing something. Doing nothing. Hollis doing.

When the clothes were safely in the closet, she fussed with her small case of jewelry. There wasn't much, but this small amount pleased her. Without looking at Hugh, she made a smooth transition to removing the jewelry she had on and placing it carefully on the table. She slipped off her shoes and nudged them under the bed. She walked to the closet again and took off her blouse. Hugh is now puzzled. What is she doing? He looked at his watch. 11:37 in the morning.

Hollis seemed to Hugh to be lost in a small dream of her own, yet her movements were very deliberate, as they had been when she was unpacking her bag. She now had her skirt hung on the clips provided on the hangers in good hotels and inns. She turned to him in her slip, and neatly pushed the straps to the side and the slip fell in a perfect silk puddle. His eyes were glazed with her in a bra and panties looking at him with a wan smile, as if she was the Mona Lisa of the western coast of Vancouver Island, the sea's own prelude to the storm. Could this be the easy calm that preceded the Big One?

She walked again to the night stand with the lamp that had her jewelry, and looking at him, took off first her panties and then the bra. She was motionless. Her smile remained. Her own lack of motion had caused him to become struck as well.

His eyes did not blink, but his mind was a whirl of unexpected emotions. She had said in New York, some days ago now, that the deal would be she wouldn't sleep with him. Of course he was wondering how to resettle that idea in her mind, so that he would be free to settle himself on her body. This was some lovely body Hollis had. Lord of Storms, what a body… slim, pert, clearly alive in all senses of the word. The details were there as well. The breasts that invited all sorts of touching and tasting. Greenish eyes that now were glaring at him. Was there a dare there? Not sure. The blondish bush standing out from the Y in her body, and to distract him, she shook her hair at the moment she saw his eyes move down on her. So now his look was back into her eyes.

There was no movement in the room for several minutes while Hugh sorted through his mind what might be the meaning of this, while she stood to reveal the whole of herself to him.

"I wanted you to see. So, you wouldn't wonder." she said.

"Uh, yes, well, what can I say…you are gorgeous…even delicious. Thank you."

Another long pause between them. Finally, he heard what she had said, "What do you mean that I shouldn't wonder?"

"I know that guys want to know what you look like, stripped. They want to see it."

"Well," he stammered. He was not used to this, this stammering, and it unnerved him. He was not used to being unnerved. He seemed to have what he wanted, but what, he wondered was keeping him from taking it. It was Hollis who was keeping this from him while openly offering it, wasn't it?

"Well, of course, we want to see something this wonderful, what guy wouldn't?"

"I thought it might help you."

The final cue. Hugh got up and moved toward her. "Sure. Sure does. Saves me all that trouble of, ah, helping you take them off."

"…so, that you might not have to wonder what it was that you would not be getting." Hugh stopped in mid-pace. "That's what I mean. I think one of the important things to guys is that they see it, they want to know what you look like. That's part of it. So, if you are not going to have the whole dishy, then at least you will be able to see it, me…"

"…ah, we aren't going to…ah, lie down together…? Is that what you mean?"

"Yes."

"Any reason we are not?"

"You said I didn't have to fuck you."

"Yeah, well, we were in New York then. Now we are in…" and he turned to the broad window with its spectacular view of the sea and the channel islands nearby. "Now were are in this great place. We are here together to have a good time. So, I assumed that you would want to…"

"...fuck you because you have me in this "great place?" And, you are man, I am a girl, and that's all it takes." She paused to lean into him with a hard glance. "No, no, you also have all this money and good looks and, what's a girl to do faced with That?"

They were five feet from each other. A fully dressed man, good looking with all that money. A fully undressed, she had called herself a "girl," but this was a fulsome woman. Neither one of them moved. His bags were unpacked on the bed. The closet to his right was stocked with her clothes. The view behind them was heartbreaking. All she could think to say, as her shoulders and breasts made an almost unnoticeable shrug was,

"Some crappy deal, eh..."

What a remarkable scene, thought Janet. I know it's not the first in the novel Kellnur was trying to write, but it is quite powerful in terms of, what, setting the stage in this place where they have come... and the relationship struggle that insues, as well as the possiblity of some sort of a transformation of character. Plus, what a brave thing for a woman to do, take your clothes off, not in a sexy way, but calmly, patiently, to show you will not be intimidated into something that will compromise you.

Janet drifted into a reverie, sitting on the end of the bed and wondered what *she might look like* doing a stunt like that... taking off her clothes to show a man —- that's where her thoughts fell off the track. She had been with a man... three men to be exact, and she tried to settle her mind on what she and he had done, and how. She had never, would never reveal herself to a man that way, and at the same moment, she wondered what her body might look like, have looked like to Paul or Lance or... and her mind stopped. What was she thinking? How could she think like that! She was a proud woman, wasn't she, and this was a novel, a story invented by a man who is inventing the woman, the woman he wants to portray... yet that doesn't mean that a woman wouldn't DO that or act in a, well, the woman wasn't trying to be provocative. In a another way, she was being most protective.

Janet couldn't decide, in this second reading of this part of the novel… she would not have thought of herself in that way – but, it was a story, wasn't it. Yet she did find it provocative, and wondered if… yes, wondered if she could be that way with a man. As well has how she might look, totally nude in a room with a strange man… or maybe even a man she knew.

But, wait, Janet, she thought, you are reading this to find out the flow of the story, where it is going, what's going to happen so that you may be able, some how, to determine what the ending of this will be in Kellnur's mind…

Maybe it was time to concentrate on another aspect of Kellnur and his story. Yes. As a distraction, let's find another poem and then quit for the day…

…this looks promising…

1000 Stars

There is a man who lives deep in the heavens.

Every night he counts the stars.

He does this because
he loves to live through the black night
in the light of the stars. And, he loves to count, so…

Every night there are 1000s of stars to count, and the man is happy.

If one star is missing, he searches all night long
to insure that star is found, shining and safe.

Every star is important.

Well, that's a good note to go home on… perhaps even to count the stars overhead tonight and muse on them, it's nice to know that there is an "assistant editor-in-the-sky" who keeps track of things up there… Janet wondered if she might be able to figure out something in-the-sky… like Chapter 15. Oh my. What fun!

The Search for Kellnur Truth

It was the end of the first week of Janet's, as she began to call it, "search for Kellnur truth" that she was able to collect the three most significant "sub-truths."

First of all, she had been listing and categorizing all of Kellnur's work… that is poems, now-that-she-discovered-he-was–a-decent poet; short stories and novel fragments… her listing was comforting because to her it was beginning to draw an image of the man-as-writer. In the midst of this, she found that he was trying to organize a book of his short stories. This being done in the usual fashion of writers that have a semi-name or are beginning to have a body of work. She had always wondered if the short stories of this fashion were not a shield or cover for the fact that other longer projects were bogged down. Was this the case with Kellnur? Why there was no Chapter 15, or was it here and she couldn't find it… or a sudden thought: had Kellnur taken it with him in the hopes of making it better, more interesting or, or, or? Nope, just think it's here!

The second discovery led to the third: she found three letters from a woman in Denver named Jennifer Kohl. This lady was writing notes to Kellnur in the manner of a budding writer trying to get a handle on what she was trying to do and how to do it — asking Kellnur for advice on a novel idea she had. These notes seemed to be left hanging in mid-air until she found a photo of this woman signed to "Joseph, the miracle worker" attached to a check stub for $10,000.

What? What had she missed here! That's a great deal of money! She was sitting on the edge of the bed in the main room, trying to catch her breath and her racing mind. The woman in the picture was youngish, mid-thirties and attractive, standing in front of a statue of a man… no clue as to who the man was. Perhaps some Denver hero?

The check stub glared at Janet as if to say, "…so you think you know what's going on here?" She could almost hear the laughter of the photo of the woman and the money. Suddenly, she wondered if Kellnur had been to Denver to help her, if he had actually helped or worse-better, writ-ten something for this woman… and then, idly, had she slept with Joseph? A lot of questions that will have no answer, unless… unless she could find some proof or evidence that he had… what is the word… become a ghost-writer for this woman and her novel idea.

Ghostwriter. Well, hadn't Kellnur talked about how no one plans to be a ghost — maybe this is the foundation of his remark. He had never planned to be a Ghostwriter. She had heard of these arrangements, but in fact, knew little about them, how they come to be and why a person would write something for someone else and not use your own real name. This was a fairly good-sized problem in Janet's mind until she suddenly realized that there may be something right here in front of her that said something about Jennifer Kohl that she had glazed over, thinking it was nothing. Now, it was some-thing.

She began to conduct a sweeping search for other papers signed or named Jennifer Kohl, or Jennifer or, oh, no! Not JK, My God, what's going on here? Another JK… Janet stood in the middle of the Table Room and felt dizzy and thought to arrest the feeling by standing stock still for 30 seconds and then sitting in the chair by the small bookcase. She needed to gain some balance and perspective here. She looked out the window to the River and wondered if it wouldn't be a good idea to go out for a breath. As her eye glazed a small bookcase under the window, she saw a colorful book jacket with an odd title: **The Scissors of Matisse**.

The Scissors of Matisse by Jennifer Kohl

She stared at it as if it was a ghost. As if it might move off the shelf of its own accord and leap into her hands, demanding that she, the Kellnur Recorder of Truths, add this to The Document. That is, to the body of work attributed to the un-famous ghostwriter, Joseph Kellnur. Oh, my God…

She reached for the book and opened it to the back of the jacket cover. There was the same picture of Ms. Jennifer Kohl, the JK of dreams. It said this was the first novel of Ms. Kohl, who was a lecturer of literature at Denver University and the wife of Jacob Kohl, recently deceased, prominent Denver business person.

The front jacket flap revealed the story of the book.

This sensuous story is the debut novel of Jennifer Kohl of Denver University, and what a lovely story it is.

The Scissors of Matisse tells the story of Alec Knowles, a widower trying to drown the sorrows of losing his wife who has recently died. He has run away to the west coast of California, has traded his prized possession, the actual scissors used by Matisse to create his famous "cut out art" for this land and house teetering on the edge of the famous cliffs of Big Sur, that strip of land famous for its hanging beauty on the coast of California.

The story is full of picturesque, Big Sur scenes as well the love affair between Knowles and a woman who comes to his aid when he cuts off a finger in his amateur work building, an unnecessary birds' nest for the flights of sea birds circling his home. One of the delights of this story is Knowles feeding frenzy of the birds who become his best neighbors, like the woman who comes to share his bed along with the dread of her abusive husband.

This is a must-read for its ironic happenings, lovely images of the coast and a rather different love story.

Well, she had the book in her hand… why not a quick read of some of his ghost writing for another JK… Let's start with the "birdhouse scene on the cliffs of Big Sur…"

Paul was up early. Excited to be productive in his new home and environment.

He brought the radio outside and found a good music station on the radio. He liked classical music and there were two channels to choose from. Extension cords were hooked up at the kitchen power supply and lines run outside the house to operate the tools and the radio.

Paul took himself out to the edge of the cliff and looked down toward the rocks and small beach. If he had been a religious man, he would kneel there and thank whoever was responsible for his good fortune — and wished only that his good wife, now deceased, was there with him, to smile on his madness and to make the onion soup he liked for lunch.

His work on building this rack of birds' nests had gone well. The nests were anchored to four by four posts already in the ground. The rails proceeded upward from there. Small shallow boxes were placed on each level, and, as planned, each level was offset from the one below. In a way, the whole of it looked, as it was formed like a rack of music shaped in space, as if the birds in flight settling there might be the notes of a great Concert on Wings.

Paul was on the ladder putting in the last railing with the power saw when the balance of man, lumber and blazing tool slipped out of control. Paul heard himself scream as if some terrible element had pierced his body, and it had… The saw had missed the railing and cut off the last finger on his left hand. As he heard himself scream, he watched the finger fall away from him, trailing blood in a double stream, one from the falling finger, one from the severed place on his hand. He stood frozen for a second and then dropped the power saw, still spinning. It hit the ground ripping and drove itself several feet before catching on a rock and chipping to a stop.

Paul was watching his finger when he heard her. "Please, please," said this voice, "...please come down and let me look at your finger." He looked to the bottom of the ladder and there was a woman, as if she had grown out of his lost finger. Where could she have come from? She took a tentative step up the ladder and held out her hand to him. Should there have been another observer to the scene, looking from a distance, the sight was bizarre: the man at the top of the ladder, the woman as a supplicant below the man, who is still attached by wire to the tool at the edge of the cliff, all of this as notes on the bird racks. A second concerto, for Birds, Lost Fingers and Lunatics.

She coaxed him off the ladder onto the ground. "My name is Sarah. I walk here often in the early morning. I heard you scream and I came." It sounded so natural.

In the house, she was quite efficient. Found bandages, wound them around his hand and taped them so pressure would stop the bleeding. She was a plain woman, soft spoken, a well-shaped face with thin lips wearing no make up. She wore a shapeless dress in the fashion of women who had bad legs or who were heavier than they wished, as if she might be trying to hide something ...

So, Joseph Kellnur is further revealed. As well as another JK. I wonder what's happened to her, and if she knows that Kellnur is missing, or even easier, *is he there with her* now that she is a new widow? Well, that would be worth a phone call or two. Janet made a note to follow up on this over the weekend. And, perhaps a bit of homework as well... a quick read of The Scissors of Matisse. A thin first novel with an uncredited writer — no, no, no... a very real Ghostwriter in the background.

What am I to make of this? thought Janet. This is major and she began to wonder how or even if she should reveal this to Jonas Keppleman, my God... she could hear the gasps and see the rolled eyes. Their new dis-appeared hero, Joseph Kellnur, is now a ghostwriter for some woman in Denver and her small novel, not reviewed in the New York Times! What to do?

She looked at her watch. It's late, time to call it a day and a week and a novel discovery. She lay back on the bed in the living-sleeping room and rested her eyes. What was to become of her, the honest person sent to find The Lost Chapter of the novelist Joseph Kellnur and — by the by, what happened to him, where is he, is he on yet another ghostwriting gig and why had he slept with the widow of, what was his name, Knowles, yes, Jacob Knowles… Yet another JK to add to our growing list of supernatural initials. She was already tired and this finished her off — she was past tired, and she nodded off to sleep in Kellnur's bed.

When Janet roused herself enough to realize where she was, not at home in her own bed, she turned over and pulled the covers over her shoulders and settled down for a real night's sleep… perhaps the light of day would bring peace and clarity. How she longed for clarity and peace as she fell asleep.

Janet looked out of the window down to North Michigan Av-enue and the elegance of Chicago and said out loud…

"So, this is Mt. Everest and…"

"…it's not in Tibet, or the IMAX movie place down the street, it's right here in the third largest city in America."

She turns away from the window view to see a man… tallish, dressed casually, and looking intently at her. "So, you are the fabled Janet Kidder… I am so pleased to meet you." His hand was out-stretched toward her. She took it.

"…and you, Sir, are you a visiting publisher to the party here, looking for a new book? or could you be the newest up and coming Nelson Algren, or…?"

"…sorry that you have guessed wrong, but then, how could

you know? But, first things first, I want you to know how grateful I am to you and your publishing company... but mainly to you, because as good as Jonas is, I know it is YOU who have made the difference." He gestured beyond the balcony of the highly placed restaurant overlooking the city... Mt. Everest of Chicago. "So, the stars in the sky and I wish to honor you. I won't kneel here in front of you so as to attract unwanted attention, but I want to give you the attention you deserve after the party, if you will be so kind as to join me later... and, now that I see you in person, how lovely you are, and how wise and discreet you are, I realize my additional good fortune."

There was a pause between them. Janet didn't know what to say, but the man did.

"Please let me introduce myself, I am Joseph Kellnur and I would like to invite you up to my home on the North Branch of the Chicago River and hope you would be willing to put aside all normal conventions and let me add myself to your sleep tonight in my bed, where I know you have enjoyed your lonely, lovely self. Tonight it will be different if you will, how shall I say, embrace me there."

"Oh my God... it's... you are... ooohhhh..." ...and Janet turned in Kellnur's bed to feel the burning sun race into the windows of his apartment, as she was coming out of a deep, deep, dreaming sleep...

"OooooooooooooooomyGod, what a dream, I hope." Janet sat up and looked around Kellnur's living-working-sleeping room to be certain she was alone... "...but now I am dreaming about him, no less... ohhhhh, dear is this beginning to be the loss of any control I have over..."

...she pulled herself up in the bed pushing the pillows behind her to sit up and consider what was really happening here. She has made the simple mistake of falling asleep — for the night — in his bed and now she dreams that he has asked her to... join him!

She would have given much to have the bedroom where it should be, overlooking the river, so that she could collect her thoughts, dreams and some sort of balance. She smiled, well, I guess fair is fair, here I am invading his life, home and inner writer's thoughts, and now he is reciprocating by invading my dreams. As she lay there, she tried to re-create enough of the dream to see herself and him in this place downtown that she had only heard of... what did Joe Kellnur look like... think now, Jannie, you SAW him, what does he look like... shouldn't you know this about a man you have never met who has just invited you to a roll in the... oh, yes, she smiled here:

a roll in the ether

he is the ghostwriter   and   you are the Ghost, oh my...
...must be time for coffee and a plan for the day...please, yes, a plan.

DAY SEVEN
41 Wives

Janet slipped into the kitchen and made herself coffee. Yes, that was more like it. Trying physically to shake herself awake and away from "the dream." Yes, it will always be referred to thus, *The Dream*.

She marveled again at how neat the kitchen was in such contrast to the rest of the apartment. Coffee cup in hand... she wandered idly through the apartment as if it was her first visit. A quick glance at the bed to be certain it had been *The Dream*. No need to take notes of this for later. The coffee cup in her hand was shuddering, so she made a physical effort to gain control over her body — a trembling hand will make it difficult to take notes on what she was observing — trying to gain some control over her thoughts and get a fresh insight on this world class puzzle she was drowning in. Remembering that there were not many photos, and no family pictures... she paused for a moment in the midst of this to see if she could recall an image of the man in her dream —com'on, Jannie, get a grip, it's either time to get organized for another day or take the day off and go to the movies. What to do?

She wondered if she would ever complete this assignment and go back to the comfort of her office on Sixth Avenue and the pleasures of life in New York and her hopes... yes, she had hopes. Try not to forget your hopes to one day be a Kellnur and write a novel, one in which all the pages and chapters are there to turn over to the publisher.

In the middle of trying to re-create a new awake Janet Kidder, she took a new look at the apartment and its stacks and stacks... and she found another box that was under the short table by the front windows. She hadn't seen that before, so she opened it to more color file folders. The box was titled

41 Wives

...inside were numbers and names of women. Mmmm, provocative title... she sat down and wondered if this was going to be another coastal birds' rack only this time in a different part of the world. But not to forget this may be the distraction the morning dreams called for... what-is-this?

7. (Did that mean Wife #7?)

Janice, Janice, Janice. After all these years, nearly 20, I still think of Janice. It's odd how the fabric of a memory catches on the rusty nail of your mind and just flutters there. It's even odder that this did not begin, this fluttering, until years later and as if submerged, Janice floated to the surface. Whole. Bright. Blonde, with grey eyes and light skin that burned easily in the sun. A voracious reader of books that mattered. Because she was married to another man, we only talked about the things that mattered and books were top of the list. I would watch her with him. She would watch me with Catherine. We were lucky that it was not the other way around.

We got away with much, Janice and I. In a way it frightened me. I wondered what might happen? I had never made love to another man's wife. Even more frightening, I had never made love to another man's wife in his bed. Some perversity in her seemed to like that the best, though in a way there was no best for her. She was even, level and straight. I thought her to be a better person than I.

Well, yes, thought Janet, it's like the bird cages on the edge of the world only this time it's wives on the edge of the living room... maybe it was time to quit — Take **41 Wives** home to read and think about this in relation to all she had learned… well, what had she learned anyway?

And, where was the XFMFGAAA Chapter? Oooohhhhhh…

In the car on her way home, Janet's cell phone rang.

"Hi, Jannie… where are you?"

"In a state."

"You traveling?"

Janet smiled… yes, that must be it.

The voice continued, a very familiar voice.

"I called your office and they said you were here, in Chicago somewhere. Are you somewhere close enough to have lunch, I have been worried about you."

What a good idea, thought Janet finally recognizing the voice of her long lost best friend, Hanna — and Hanna lived in Chicago now. They made arrangements to meet in 20 minutes at a place that Janet could easily find.

The two women might have been twin sisters, except that they were three years apart in age and they were not sisters, but long time best friends. Janet was 31 and Hanna was 34. Both semi-blond naturally, both with smiling green eyes and both thin. Hanna came in jeans. Janet had not succumbed to "jeans" and thus was the odd one here…

"No jeans!"

"No, thank you."

"…so this is sounding like a very interesting assignment. Do you mind that it's different than your usual work?" Hanna was nothing if not diplomatic, she had been after her best friend to, as she spoke of it, break out of the past and join the 21st Century. What a good idea!

Janet, patiently oblivious to the prodding said, "Well, as you have heard, Joseph Kellnur is a pretty interesting man."

"How old is he? Is he good looking?"

Janet wondered if this was the moment to bring up *The Dream*. Hmmmm, maybe later, maybe never. She continued, "There are no pictures of him… oddly, not even in the fly jacket of his book… and no pictures almost at all in his apartment. So, I don't have a clue."

"Hmmmm, odd… well, it certainly sounds interesting. Could I have one of these secret manuscripts to read?" Janet hesitated… what should she say here? "Oh, why not, Hanna… maybe you can help me determine what kind of a man is Kellnur and therefore, how he might finish this book we are trying to publish… or even better, find him!"

"I'd love to. Maybe we should become some kind of Detective Sisters and see if we can find him," Hanna smiled. Janet nodded.

"…well, yes, we did that once before didn't we… ha-ha, the Detective Sisters." She reached her hand across the table to take Hanna's. It was so good to have a close friend… especially right now.

"Let's be serious for a moment," said Hanna, "Even though this is not going well… I hear that it's different and interesting, worthwhile… all that stuff that's about living a life worth living. For instance, all this sounds like there could be more here, because this man is, what shall we say, more than ordinary?"

"Yes, he is more of an iceberg than an island, yet, his not being present presents more than a mystery… but what is your thought?"

"It sounds like you should be writing a novel about him… that this might be your big chance… after all, you work for a publishing company in New York… they are always looking for unique concepts —" Hanna paused to let that sink it… she was always saying things like this. Then, "What about it, Jannie, isn't it time to come out of the closet?"

"Yes, yes…" Sigh. "Yes." A sip of coffee, a look out the window, then…

"What is it that makes you think I can do this?" A stage pause, then, "Will you help me?" Hanna nods, smiles and says… "OK then, let's make a plan… and the first step might be to see if we can find Kellnur by going to visit the two women."

"Two women?"

"Yes, Darling," said Hanna, "the two woman you have discovered in Kellnur's life."

"Oh, those two…"

"Yes, and isn't it helpful that Denver and Windsor… across the river from Detroit, aren't too far away."

"How long do you think that might take?" asked Janet.

"Well, we can get to Detroit in a day of driving, Denver is further. I don't know, maybe we only need to talk to one of them… you make it sound like he seemed closer to the lady in Windsor… and if I had to guess, once the book was done for the woman in Denver, and they had their final lovemaking, my guess would be that it-was-o-v-e-r."

"That sounds right. Isn't it odd, we are acting here like we know, absolutely "know" Joe Kellnur… and I'll bet that can't be true, having been in his place for more than a heavy week, I feel certain that I don't know, how shall I say it, the real Kellnur (even though we woke up together this very morning.) Wish I did, maybe I could write the last chapter."

"What a concept," said Hanna.

"Ha-ha…"

"All I know, is that I want to read his novel… all but the last chapter, of course… can I do that tonight?"

"Sure, I have it at the place I am staying… let's go over there…"

After a light dinner, they went to the apartment where Janet is staying and she gave the manuscript (thus far) to Hanna, who immediately dived into it… murrmuring and nodding from time to time. It got late, so Janet fussed with her notes while Hanna finished up the book.

"Well, I like this…" said Hanna. "…good images, nice smooth text. My fave scene is the one where the artist, Kerry Cox, finds the small island off the beach and goes there."

"I like that part too. But, aren't you impressed with Kellnur's depiction of the beach at Tofino?"

"Absolutely! It's hard to think of a beach that vast… feels more like a desert than a sand patch that borders an ocean. Plus how the two couples take that walk together and they seem to get lost in that very vastness, where the ocean is both near to them and far, too."

"So, what did you say your fave part was?" Janet asked.

"Where the artist finds and goes to this small island with all the brambles, trees, a small forest… and it feels to him like he is in his own brain — so complex, so winding the paths, so deep and mysterious. I mean, don't you love it?"

"I do — hand it to me…"

Janet flipped through the pages to where the artist, Kerry Cox, moves into the tunnels of this tiny island he calls The Brain…maybe even his brain…

"…inside this small Rock island, there is jungle-like tangle, this is at the south end of MacKenzie Beach… maybe the widest beach in the world… and what a world! thought Kerry.

…roots and fallen trees are the main inhabitants of this place. Not a place you can just walk through. I found a tunnel, really, up into it and then it twists around and into the small island. Black rock lines the edges. Inside, God knows how many trees crowded together. It seems like the whole interior place is roots, up turned, forming loops to trip over, hand holds to grab, moss on them… quite picturesque in fact…yet in another way, it feels like one has just managed to crawl inside one's head, directly to the brain path."

"What a thoughtful idea… makes me tired…" said Hanna, "…too much brain work." They laughed.

"Well, let's call it a night."

They retired to the only bedroom in the place and slipped into bed. Janet in her nightgown, and Hanna in her slip, less the bra and panties. They curled together like the sisters they thought they were and fell fast asleep.

In the morning, Hanna was up first and in the kitchen figuring out how to make coffee for the two of them. She clattered around quietly until she had it all together. As she sits on the edge of the bed, Janet comes to and looks up to find a coffee cup almost in her hand.

"Now this is what I call Room Service. Got a croissant to go with all this?" Janet smiled at Hanna.

"Nope, that French guy didn't turn up this morning, and I can't make muffins in a strange kitchen."

"Well, allll right…"

"So," said Hanna, "Literary Detective #1, what's your thought and plan for the day?"

"I thought we'd hop over to that equipment place and rent a Literature X-Ray Machine for the day and program it to show us all the hidden manuscripts."

"I like it. Ha-ha-ha"

"Well, to be more practical, let me take you over to his apartment and show you the place. Maybe you will see something that I have missed. Let's call it the Scene-of-the-Crime."

"Ha, ha, yes, let's…"

Action is Indicated, she said...

Janet was pleased to see that Hanna was as overwhelmed by Kellnur's place as she had been that first day. This seemed to validate the absolute complexity of her assignment. Hanna walked through the rooms touching everything... was as wordlessly fascinated with the bedroom-writing-working-filing space as Janet had been. Then, the mysterious Table Room with its circle of mysteries. But, very early in this investigative and ruminating walk, Hanna found the notes and cards from the two women... Ms. Denver and Ms. Windsor.

"You know, Jannie, I think action is indicated here." She pointed to the wall of two women. "Why not call one of them and ask for Joe Kellnur and see what happens... not to jump to conclusions, let's start with the woman Kellnur wrote for in Denver?"

Janet was startled. It took a moment and then she said, "Course, why not... I should have thought of that... ah, which one do you think?"

"I think it would be best to start with the woman who didn't write him love notes.'

"Fine, I think her information is here somewhere..." Janet fished around the desk across from the bed and found it... "Here we are, a phone number for Jennifer Knowles."

"Great," said Hanna, looking around. "Does his phone still work?"

"Never tried..."

Hanna picked up the phone and got a dial tone and handed it to Janet. Paper in one hand, phone in the other, she dialed. What she noticed as she dialed was that she hadn't thought of what to say, so when the other end answered, Janet said very naturally, "Oh hi, I'm trying to reach Joe Kellnur — he told me you and he were friends...is he there, or could you help me find him?"

Janet held the phone out for Hanna to hear. A pause on the other end, and finally… "Ah, Miss, I'm not sure who you are or why you are calling, but I don't know a… what did you say the name was Joe Keller?"

"Ah, no, it's KellNUR… I mean Joe… surely you remember him?"

"Not only do I not remember him, as you say, but I have never known a Joe Kell-nur… you must have a wrong number."

"But I was certain…"

"I'm sure it was a simple mistake, a wrong number or something, but I can't help you because I don't know a Mr. KellNUR… best of luck…" and the line went dead.

Janet held the phone out to Hanna to hear the dial tone buzzing. Hanna shook her head in wonder, "but you said you have all the proof that Kellnur worked for her… Wasn't there a check for a lot of money? and a book…" Hanna looked around as if the book might be right there in front of them.

"I can't believe it!" said Janet, "…how could this woman act like that after all the proof we have here…" Janet slumped back and Hanna could hear her unspoken words: "This is Impossible!"

"What a dead-end!" Hanna was bewildered. "I guess from what you said, we might expect a different answer than, go-get-lost and have a good day."

Janet sat down on the end of the bed, Hanna looked at her in that pose and set the phone down to come to sit beside Janet. "Not to worry, honey, there is still that other woman on the other side of Detroit… what is her name… maybe we learned something here… let's not call anyone. Not on the phone with this lady. Let's go to Windsor and SEE This Lady, in person, on the door step and ask for Kellnur. Surely, she can't say no, maybe we even take one of her love letters to hand to her in case she gets difficult."

Janet nodded and lay back. "You're right, Detective #2, that's a plan." Hanna lay back with her. "If you are a good detective, you've always got an option, right?"

"Right."

"Let's get a road map to Detroit and see how that could work." A pause.

Another dead-end, thought Janet, but this time I am not in this alone… how good it was to have someone right beside you when you are lost in the woods… and The Joe Kellnur Woods were pretty deep and dark. She closed her eyes and reached over to hold Hanna's hand.

The drive to Detroit went fast… but the new map quest problem was how to find this woman's house in Windsor… they had dinner at this nice place with a view of the River Rouge — what a cute name for this industrial river — and studied the map, as well as asking the waitress if there was a good place to crash for the night.

Yes, there was.

Right on the river was a place with a cute name, The Red Rooms, and one of them overlooking the river… the River Rouge they reminded themselves.

They had picked up a couple of cans of beer and as luck would have it, there was a small balcony to their room right on the river. They sat there and thought through the next day. Janet said they should be very casual in their approach to Carleen Bathhurst. She wouldn't be an "agent" from a publishing house, but a close writer friend of Joe's — they actually started calling him "Joe" as if they were old college buddies. Turns out that Jannie was being mentored by Joe and now he's gone from Chicago. Jannie is desperate for his help with the writing she is doing… does Carleen know where Joe is… better, is he here with her?

Yes, that worked, they both agreed to this "script" and the flow and sense of it. They would dress down so they wouldn't seem official and they would seem friendly. So, they had a plan.

"…and I am ready to call it a day…"

"Me, too."

The two of them moved into their room, and took turns at the bathroom sink to wash faces and brush hair. Janet was the first in bed, a queen sized one that would fit them both. She turned off the light on her side, waiting for Hanna to join her. What a help and Godsend she had been… they were actually making some headway here — who knows what could happen tomorrow — and it was fun for a change instead of always-the-big-mystery.

Hanna came out of the bathroom in her slip and crawled into bed beside Jannie and turned off the light. They lay there together in the dark, lost in the thoughts of the coming day — wouldn't it be a marvelous turn of events if Kellnur WAS there and the mystery was solved — they would get the Last Chapter. Janet turned over and as she did, she felt Hanna move over alongside her. It was good to have a friend and partner in a deep mystery, and she said, "Hanna, honey, it's great that you are here to help me and helped-you-have… thanks so much." She felt Hanna's hand on her shoulder and it seemed to slide down her body, inside her slip until Hanna had her hand over Jannie's breast… and then her fingers touched Jannie's soft nipple. Jannie felt her own double reaction… first a shudder and then a slight movement of her body melding into Hanna's body. It seemed a dream of breasts, Hanna's hand on hers and her back into Hanna's breasts… she hadn't noticed that Hanna had slipped away from her slip as she was getting into bed. Now they were here, together, truly together, melded as two true friends.

It felt so good and she turned to Hanna to give her a deep kiss… lips to lips and breasts to breasts.

The next morning, Jannie was facing the window to the river, she wished she could lie in bed and actually see the river. She wanted to turn over to see Hanna, but she was afraid of waking her. But, slowly, almost imperceptibly, she did turn herself to see Hanna, and there she was, awake and staring off into the far ceiling.

"Hi…" said Jannie.

"Oh, you're awake… I didn't want to get up for fear of tumbling you out of your dream."

Janet smiled at her. "Well, it seems that we lived our dream before sleep last night — wait —" she said as Hanna began to speak in what would be a concerned voice… "How did you feel about our night together?"

Hanna looked at her, trying to find balance, "Well, I felt fine about our night together, but I worry that I may have thrown what is a wonderful and fine relationship out of skew… ah, balance…"

"…and so did I feel fine about our… night together… if we can call it that. Look, Hanna, we have been friends for more years than we can count or remember

— and, yes, I was surprised, most surprised that you touched me and kissed me last night... but we went to sleep in peace, and I think we need to leave it at that. I don't feel a need for an examination or apology or deeper discussion... in fact, I don't think anything need be said. We have been friends for years and last night we were just closer friends."

Hanna looked as if she had been struck in the face with a soft bag of marshmallows. And then she deflated, and seemed to fall into herself. She reached her hand out to touch Jannie's face. "Oh, thank you, thank you, Jannie, for not scolding me or hating me or... oh, whatever... I didn't think this out in the bathroom last night while I washed my face... I didn't even realize I slipped off my slip," they both smiled at this. " I just did... I guess it's something I have always wanted to do. I wanted to touch you, and have you touch me. I am hoping, guessing, that it felt good to us both... so there..." Hanna smiled and Jannie pulled her closer and kissed her again.

"Yes it felt good, and thankfully we don't have to write a 500 page essay to turn in this afternoon," Jannie said, pulling down the bed sheet... "and to prove I mean it, you can kiss and touch my boobs again, right now... oookay..."

Hanna leaned over and kissed Jannie's breasts, both of them.

"See, nothing happened except that I can tell you that felt good. I don't think we need more of a talk or reason than that... thank you, Hanna..." and Jannie leaned into Hanna and kissed her. Pulling back she said, "Allllll riiight, let's get up and go see this woman and hope to heaven that she can point us to the room Kellnur is in or the direction he went toward... Okay?"

Hanna had pulled back from Jannie with a show of small wonder on her face. "Ooookay."

They got up, each on her side of the bed, and got dressed to face the... what would they be facing today?

It was a nice neighborhood about three blocks from the river. Janet noticed that proximity and wondered about the Coincidence of Rivers... hmmm, another good title... she and Hanna mounted the steps to this white house and knocked on the door. Presently, the door opened and there was a lovely woman with long brown hair in a dressing gown.

"Yes…?"

"We are wondering if you can help us find Joseph Kellnur, we are writing students of his who are just happening to be passing by."

Hanna added, "Mr. K had spoken of you in class and we are on our way to the Shakespeare Festival in… ah…" Carleen finished her sentence: "…yes, in Stratford." Both the women nodded.

Then came a moment that seemed to last forever as Carleen looked these two gals up and down and smiled to herself. "Ah, why don't you come in and we can talk about it."

Janet hung back for a moment as Hanna swept by the woman in the doorway. Inside, Carleen gestured to a small alcove with a seating area. They all sat, now facing each other. Janet and Hanna waited to see what might be said next… this was feeling stranger and stranger.

"Let me guess," said Carleen, "you are not any of Joe's family, you are not here to repossess his car from the Auto Company, but you are with his publisher in New York…" Janet was stunned. "And, they are very… ah, very anxious to have the Last Chapter of Joe's new book?"

Hanna smiled at the woman. "Exactly, and we are hoping he is here or you know where he is or, maybe he even read the Chapter to you?"

"No, he didn't…"

"But, you know where he is."

"Yes, certainly," Carleen gestured around her, "he's in Canada."

The two women laughed and seemed to ease up. Obviously, this was going to be a game and it wouldn't pay to rush ahead. Better, perhaps all would be revealed. Carleen straightened her dressing gown and leaned back in her chair. "Why don't you give me a minute," she said, "there is coffee right there on the side table, why not pour yourselves a cup and let me think for a moment."

Hanna got up, gesturing for Jannie to stay put and went to the table and poured two cups of coffee, one with lots of cream and one with lots of sugar. She handed the sweet one to Jannie and smiled at her, as if this was going to be an interesting Chapter with the Detective Sisters.

Carleen came back and sat down in the cove with Janet and Hanna. "I should start by saying that I don't have it. Actually, Joe doesn't have it either." She looked squarely at Janet. "You are the one from the publisher, right?'

Janet nodded and sipped her coffee.

After another long pause, Carleen said, "…well, it's this way. I can't tell you how many times in the past few weeks we have gone over the story," and here she gestured out the window," at our lovely Vancouver Island… I just love Victoria… Have you been there?"

Hanna nodded yes, and Janet affirmed no.

"I don't have to tell you that it takes place, this story, up the west side of the Island in Tofino, by the bay there." She paused to seemingly place herself there, in Tofino, and determine what to say next, or even where to go next. The two women listeners remained relaxed and patient, waiting for the trip to begin.

"…so, this horny, New York art dealer wants to treat his successful artist and his wife to a celebration trip and someone finds an ad in the NY Times about a place on the west coast of Vancouver Island called The Inn of Storms…" here Carleen smiles to herself as if she had actually been there to watch…" they have these amazing January storms on that coast and there is this inn, the Inn of Storms, where you can bring your girlfriend, wife or whatever to sit in the comfort of this lovely Inn and watch the Pacific Ocean try to wash the place away."

Carleen smiles to herself.

"So, you have been there?" this was Hanna.

"Well, yes and no." She looked at the two women, especially to Janet, "…you have been there, right… the publisher sent you there?"

Janet shook her head no. "Wish I had, it sounds lovely, and of course both you and I have read the written pages and know what an adventure that was."

Carleen said, "…well, only Joe Kellnur would bring these two couples to this wild place to see how they would get along… I just love the intimate scenes he has created, especially the one…" here Carleen looks at them. "This was one of my favorites, but Joe realized he had to take it out, as, what did he say? It was too soon for a scene like this — but this was his idea:

The Dealer Guy convinces his "girlfriend" to come down to the beach with him and curl up together in a huge blanket and feel each other up… Carleen smiles, "What I so love about Joe's writing is its spontaneity. He doesn't plan on anything more than what I just said, but then suddenly, his fingers are typing up a storm, that is, a wind comes up and blows the blanket away and there they are, stark naked, this dumb New Yorker and his, ah, fullsome girlfriend wondering if their clothes got blown away too?"

Hanna smiles, "Wow, I guess I should be reading this book while we are waiting for Joe to finish it."

"But, I have to say that no matter Joe's wildness, aberrations and random thoughts, he is a disciplined writer and knows what has to be left out of the story."

Janet smiled and nodded.

Carleen continued, "Well, so here's the rub, you see, after Joe got the artist and the dealer in this horrendous fist fight on the edge of the ocean rising up against them, the artist knocks the dealer around until he, the dealer, falls into the storm and is lost…" here Carleen pauses for effect, " then what… he has created the best cliff hanger since Spielberg and …"

The two women knew that the next sentence was… what they came all this way to hear… Janet was trembling, "Yes, yes, what happens then?"

Carleen leaned back.

Hanna leaned forward.

Janet became terrified.

The room went silent while these three women looked at each other punctuated by looking out the window, at their hands, the ticking clock on the wall and finally, their empty coffee cups. Janet got up to fill hers and Hanna's. Carleen just looked out the window.

Finally, it was Carleen who spoke. "Bottom line, girls, I don't know what happens then. You are here because your publisher doesn't know what happens next, and … and…" Janet leaned forward in her chair, "…and Joe doesn't know what happens next. He has gone in search of his ending."

"Where?"

"He said he wasn't sure where he would find his inspiration: here in bed with me, at Stratford with his idol William Shakespeare or in Niagara on the Lake," she looked at them," ...do you know where that is?" The two girls shook their heads, "...it's across the river from Buffalo, New York, on what we call the Niagara Frontier... recall we are Canadians, and the Bernard Shaw Theatre Festival is there."

Hanna looked at Jannie and they both understood that Kellnur was not in the next room, the bedroom of this woman, waiting for them to leave so Joe and Colleen could share some morning comfort.

What to say next...?

It was Colleen. "What is the publisher saying?"

"They are distraught and angry, they want 'their' Chapter."

"...and..."

"And, I, ah We, are determined to find it... ah, to find him, Joe..."

Carleen nodded. "Well, I don't know where to send you. We talked, he and I, about who might be the best inspiration. I argued for Shakespeare, Joe thought Shaw... in the end, there was no decision and he left to find it... that is, his inspiration..." she smiled to herself, "he said he would come back... and as you might imagine, I am more focussed on him than the devilish Last Chapter."

"Well, I think," it was Hanna, "I think we need to make a, what do they call it? ... a, ah, command decision... yes, that's it,

A Command Decision

... as if we are going to decide to bomb either Stratford, Canada, or Niagara... what is that? in the Lake, Canada, or go have lunch and decide how the Last Chapter comes out... Between the three of us we might be able to figure that out... Is there a good and expensive place here to have lunch... something like The Windsor or Inspiration Point on the River where we three can make this Command Decision...?"

They settled in an ideal spot for their decision meeting: this cute, trendy place on a promontory overlooking the River Rouge, Detroit was right across the River and they were in a secluded corner to have the Command Decision Last Chapter Lunch. Janet was the last to be seated and got to see the assembled idea and smiled, wishing that Jonas Keppleman could look out of his Sixth Avenue office window and see these three women sit down to "talk about that last chapter."

Hanna said, "Well, fine, let's go 'round the table, What do you think the story is about?"

As it turned out, each of the three seemed to have her own idea of what the story was about and therefore what that Last Chapter might be…

Hanna: How about going right to a movie… what does that mean? Well, a movie guy approaches them at the Inn and says he has been watching them and he thinks this is "ripe stuff" for a film about their group and how the Dealer died and there is this cute girl left over plus the artist doesn't have a dealer anymore.

Carleen: Fun idea, but I think the writer-artist in Joe would be horrified… and remember, sooner or later he will come back to face you and the music and me and "his book." I would go either for an ending where a new man enters the picture, ah, story, to help tie up the lose ends or maybe for an ending that would speak of the transformation of the girl, Hollis, who came with the dealer. Joe was a big believer in "transformation."

Jannie: Nope, I can't go for the movie thing, but I like your ideas, especially the thought of "transformation," she smiled at Carleen… "yet, I wonder about "the overall" of the arc of the story.

Carleen: Arc?

Hanna: Well, there is "the place" and the idea of Storms, there is the artist and his wife and their loss of a Dealer for his work; there is the thought that they are here in this incredible place of Storms, and we haven't yet wrapped all that up.

Jannie put her hand on Hanna's arm, "Sweetie, it's a story, a novel and yes, we have some lessons here, for instance, don't go out in a big, ocean storm without your grappling hook (they all laugh) but, it has to have an ending worthy of the story and its author who will return some time, winking at Carleen. He has to be maybe not happy, but pleased with what we have done — God help us if he finds out we worked out the ending, the three of us at a river joint outside of Detroit."

All laugh…

Hanna asks, "I don't mean to ask difficult questions, but where was Joe headed with his novel when you last talked? She looked at Canada Lady, "I'll bet he shared that with you…"

"Well, from Joe's point of view, he wanted to tell a 'character' story, which he felt would be different from his usual work — mixed into that, and this was not clear even to him, how a transformation of character could be worked into this story and the people."

Janet was thoughtful, "But then he sets his story in a very, very visual place with a bunch of visual people and scenes… I mean, The Inn of Storms and the Brain Island and the outrageous people — they are characters, right, but the 'place' is pretty visual — I wonder if Joe got caught up in too much 'visual'?"

Carleen smiled "Well, Joe is Joe, you can take the story out of the man, but you can't take the man out of the story… if that makes sense…" They all unfolded their napkins, Hmmm, what to say… what to say…

"How about we figure out an ending that is all character," said Hanna. "Jannie, can that work?"

"I guess so… I mean we have an 'interesting story now' it's just how to end it… how to, ah, sum it up."

Carleen looked out the window and seemed be lost for a moment. Janet said, "From a publishing point-of-view, the Inn of Storms is kind of an adventure by putting four people in a place that is, how could you say it, is foreign or different to them and then see how they act or change in that place."

Carleen nodded, "…yes, that's part of it, and the part we have mentioned already, Joe trying to write a character story, but as you say, he has sort of undermined himself by providing a very strong visual PLACE that has changed the people."

"But," said Hanna, "isn't that what transformation is? as well as the way a person writes, what did you call it, a character story, by putting people in a strange character-shifting place?"

"That's good, Hanna, very good," said Janet.

Carleen nodded, "now of course it's not as simple as that... and you want a last chapter, so what are we to dream up over lunch, a character transformation leading to a resolution, or a story ending..."

"...or both," added Janet.

"...and that's a lot..." said Hanna.

All heads nodded.

"So," asked Hanna, "where are we-here-now-today trying to find our way out of Joe Kellnur's self-created maze?"

The waiter arrived at just the right moment, "What would you ladies like today?"

Without thinking, Janet said, "How about An Ending Salad!"

"Beg pardon, Miss?"

They all laughed and tried to focus on the menu to order... and after the waiter left with their order, it became a very quiet lunch, with each one of them lost in her own idea of "character"

"transformation"

"idea"

"ending"

"and Joe Kellnur."

"So,"said Hanna, "how 'bout each of us writing down, in 50 words or less, what the last Chapter should 'say' about the overall story idea."

"...yes, transform and finish the story idea," said Carleen.

Janet nudged her, "You sound like The Chapter on Being A Challenging Editor... you know, the kind everyone hates because there are no answers to The Question."

They all laughed... but no one brought out a pen to write out The

Answer in 50 words or less. This was followed by yet another long, long lull in the conversation.

It was Janet who said, as she passed out sheets of paper from her briefcase... "All righty, write down, each of you, and I will too, the "story ending you think will 'work' for the book... plenty of time." She smiled at her sisters-in-league, while offering each of them a pencil. Hanna grimaced, "Hey, you know I don't work in publishing."

Janet said, "Now's your chance, Darlin', all you have to do is fix it."

Hanna stuck her tongue out at Janet and they all laughed... and put ends of pencils in their mouths to think and think and ...

Carleen smiled and looked at the pencil on the table. "I, uh, well, I don't know how to explain this to you, but my thought is that the morning after the Art Dealer is lost at sea, the others are having breakfast looking glumly out the windows at a clearing sky and a new guest walks into the small dining room and sits at the table next to them."

Hanna and Janet now watch Carleen as if she was a new person at the table. She continues, "This man is the, ah, personification of Joe Kellnur." The others put on a "WHAT-is-she-talking-about? face."

Carleen looked directly at each one in turn, "Yes, I mean as if Joe Kellnur walked into his own novel. The waiter brings him a menu but he is stunned with the clearing storm out the window. He is caught with the view, sees the group, puts the menu down and introduces himself. 'Oh, hi, I am George Spelvin... just got in last night in the middle of the storm...'"

Janet's jaw drops, what's going on here, she's a girlfriend, not A Writer.

"...the group, in this awkward moment, and their terrified mood given the storm here last night, invite this new guest to their table. He accepts and sits down beside, ah, what's her name again?"

"Hollis," said Janet, "Hollis, the lady who was found at the Art Opening in SoHo." Carleen nods, "Yes, of course. The new fellow, George Spelvin sits next to her and smiles. She smiles back... he is a good-looking fellow, this George Spelvin."

A pause…

"Now, I am not a writer or an assistant editor in New York, but I am wondering if this is the time to introduce a new character to the story, one who is interesting, attractive and who might provide, if we could work it out, an interesting ending to the story by way of pulling all the loose ends into one." Carleen paused and fiddled with her napkin and watched her breakfast companions.

Janet was stunned. Hanna was watching, alternately, Janet and Carleen to see what would be said next. And, to save the day, the waiter arrived for the second time with the dessert menu. The three women looked at him in silence, each in their own "storm." Well, they were at the Inn of Storms in theory at least… there was water outside the window, not the Pacific Ocean but the River Rouge. There was only one clear thing: the person least qualified to write The Last Chapter had a provocative beginning for this urgent need.

They ordered dessert, nice to do something easy.

Janet felt, internally, that she should be the last one to ask questions about where this is going, but she did. "So, this is a provocative idea you have. And with all provocative ideas, they need to be committed to paper…" she lingered over the word *committed*. "Let's retire until tomorrow morning and let you," here she smiled at Carleen, "see if you can, how is it the Editors say, 'flesh out' your thought/idea and then we can get together for lunch to check in with you."

Hanna jumped in, "works for me…"

Carleen smiled, and looked down at her purse, as if the girls were there in it, looking up. She said, "All right, fine, I'll be happy to give it a try." She looked up at them, "Tomorrow then, lunch here?"

Yes, yes.

The girls felt very fortunate. They had not wanted to be in the way at Carleen's, so when she offered to have them stay at her place, Janet demurred saying that they wanted to get something on the river again. When they said that to Carleen, she suggested this lovely, balcony-laden place right up the river... didn't matter that it would cost a bunch... they were within a day or a week or so of that Last Chapter. However, Hanna noticed that Jannie was... what, anxious, nervous, something. She kept her eye on her friend.

Later that night, settled in this cozy hotel, very expensive in Canadian and American dollars, Hanna had gone down to the front desk to exchange some dollars. She returned to their room to find Jannie in tears.

"Hey, hey, what's goin' on here?" She hurried over to stand beside the bed and Jannie who continued to sob. Finally, Hanna sat beside her, holding Jannie in her arms... the tears slowed down and Hanna said, "... why don't you tell me what's the matter, Jannie. Maybe we can fix it."

"No, no one can fix this... it's already there... this could be really awful."

"Why don't you tell me about it, Honey... jus' say what you are thinking."

A long pause hung over the bed until Janet finally said, "Have you got any idea what could happen... to me, to the novel, even more to Joe Kellnur if my people in New York found out about 'our lunch' today with Kellnur's 'girlfriend?'" She looked at Hanna, with tears running down her face. "If Jonas, or that killer man, Alex Horn, found out about our luncheon here, what Carleen promised to do, and then, ohmyGod... if she wrote the Chapter and we put it in the book and someone found out — by the way, who will be the first to find out," Jannie almost screamed it out... "Mr. Joseph Kellnur."

She broke down again in sobs. Hanna had no idea what to say, except to whisper softly in her friend's ear that she loved her and it would be all right, even if she wasn't sure it would be all right.

Finally, the storm broke, as if they were at the Inn of Storms itself... well, everyone knows that storms can't last forever... forever is a long, long time… and Hanna held her friend tightly until this storm blew over. Finally, she whispered in Jannie's ear long enough, and the tears ran out, and Jannie finally stopped crying.

"I'm sorry, Hanna, I just…" said Janet until Hanna broke in.

"Nothing to be sorry about, Kid, you are in a difficult spot, and not to make lightly of it, I wish Joe Kellnur was here to take notes and put you in his damned novel as the beautiful part of the storm… no, I don't mean you are lovely when you cry… I mean this is a fucked up situation, but it seems like you are close to a solution."

Jannie started to interrupt… "Nope, I'm not through," Hanna hugged her friend tightly. "I am certain that your business, that is the business of creating stories to make people laugh or cry, is full of stuff like this… in the — what do they call it in the movies — the back-story! So, the important thing to keep on the top of your pretty head is that you are close to a solution, and we need to get to bed and some rest, praying that this girlfriend of Kellnur's can pull all asses out of the fires he has created by disappearing —" Hanna slammed her hand on the bed, "…by disappearing and letting all this… all this badness fall on you. But you and I now are going to pray all this 'works out' and maybe our prayers will be answered."

Hanna got up, pulling Jannie beside her. "…and to prove that all will be well, you and I are going to get into bed now and hug each other and send off that prayer… and that will do it! OK?"

Tear streaked, Jannie hugged her friend. "Yes, I will, yes it will, yes, yes and yes again. Thank you Hanna…"

A Luncheon Meeting in Canada

The waiter approached the table as the noon sun was flashing through the windows, gleaming also on the River Rouge. The three women were there, each smiling and looking at each other in anticipation. As if *This Was The Day.*

Carleen was the only one of the three who wasn't at full sail and full smile. But it was a new day. Not to rush her, thought Janet, who was filled with anticipation as she flashed a smile at Hanna as if to thank her once again. The women sat and considered if they should have an American brunch or a Canadian one, or should they move eyes over to the small "French part?"

"What would we order," said Hanna, "if we were in Quebec?"

Carleen said, "Ask the waiter for the French menu... this is Canada, these questions are taken seriously." She smiled at Hanna, as if to say "...you Americans!"

Hanna smiled back and said, "I was saying to Jannie last night, that there is a prize winning short story going on here... the three of us just met, new to each other, with a problem that is probably as old as Charles Dickens, trying to figure out an un-figure-out-able problem."

"It's odd you should say that," said Carleen, and the other two looked up at her in wondrous trepidation.

Ignoring their amazement, Carleen said, "Well, it's pretty simple and maybe even expected... or Plain and Simple, as Joe would say, 'time for some who-is-this-character-time.' So, we need to see who he is and it's easy because we have decided that the final and solution-making character in the book is the Author Himself." Carleen looked at the faces staring at her full of wonder, fear, hope and some other useful feelings when creating novels.

Carleen continued, unfazed. "So, I have done what we talked about yesterday — and for me, it has felt like a week at hard labor to, what was that phrase, "flesh out" the idea and see if a good beginning to the last chapter could be made... and I have it here for you... but, I would like to read it to you... hope you can bear that."

The two women nodded while looking at each other and then again at Carleen. "Go ahead, we are eager and ready."

"Good," Carleen began, "what we need in addition is a good, solid Canadian Heroine... This new fellow is a writer, right, and so he is finishing a book. What book? One of the guests at his new table asks him what he writes?"

"Well," says our new writer/guest, "my good fortune is that I have just turned my book over to my publisher in Toronto... which is why I am at the other end of the country on Holiday." He glances at Hollis. She smiles at him. "My new book is about Laura Secord." He looks around the table for some awareness of his heroine.

"Who would this Laura Secord be?" Hollis asks.

The new guest will look around the table and say evenly. "Well, we don't expect the Americans to know about our country's heroines, though interestingly, she was a heroine in our war, that is yours and ours along the Niagara Frontier in 1812."

The group nods.

"Yes, can't find anyone in America who knows or remembers the War of 1812," said George, "though our Postal Service is doing its best, they had commemorative stamps about that war a year or two ago."

"But then, tell us about this Laura Lady," said Hollis.

George fishes in his pockets and produces an envelope addressed to him in Vancouver. This envelope, which he passes around the table, has a stamp honoring Laura Secord.

"Isn't that something," said Hollis with a touch of admiration in her voice. "Nothing like a man who writes novel-love-letters to his heroine." George turned to smile at Hollis. "Thank you, ah…"

"I am Hollis."

"Yes, of course…"

As if a chorus of voices, "We'd like to read your novel… is that, ah, possible?"

"Well, yes and no… is, I guess, the proper answer. The book is done and the proper copy is with my publisher in Toronto, but I have a very rough copy with me if you'd like to delve into it for an hour or so…"

General nods around the table and Hollis raised her hand, "I'd like to be first. Can I look at it first?"

"Certainly, if you'll be good enough to share… with your mates, I mean."

"Yes indeed, I can share…"

"Not to change the subject, but you all seem a bit glum… is there a problem with your visit to Canada?"

If silence and gloom can rise over a dining table, this was the moment. No one knew what to say, and finally Hollis spoke up… "…why don't I take, our new friend, Mr. Spelvin, for a walk along this amazing beach?" Her two companions nodded and Hollis got up with George Spelvin, almost transfixed, right behind her.

Carleen paused in her reading of last night's "Last Chapter Try." "I hope I haven't lulled you two to sleep with my odd and crazy ramblings — we keep saying that I am not the writer here. And, in case you are wondering, we are going to assume that Hollis takes our new George off to explain how Hugh Kinkaid fell into the storm."

"OK, OK, don't stop," said Janet, while Hanna sat, dumbstruck.

"Well, I don't know what's come over me… you know with certainty that I have never done this before. My only advantage here is that Joe's novel is set in Canada, I am a Canadian, and so I thought, perhaps we need a Canadian solution." Carleen let that rest on the table while the two women gawked at her, forkfulls of food in front of them.

Before, either Janet or Hanna could answer, Carleen jumped into the center again... "But, I am dead wrong here." She did not pause for effect, "...and dead right at the same time — I feel that this is not a good idea for an ending... by itself!" Carleen paused for effect, and then continued, "I can hear Joe saying it to me now... '...you are not kidding with this dumb idea are you, Darling,' and he would touch me caringly, 'but this can work... if we add to it — make this guy someone new to wrap up all the elements that have to come together to finish the chapter, story and ideas.'"

Janet and Hanna looked out the window to the river to make sure it and them were still here.

Then all three looked at each other and turned back to the meal at hand, as if it, the meal, was the reason they were there.

Carleen remained calm as a clam, and said, "Can we retire to my place and talk about this some more?"

"Sure," said Janet, while Hanna nodded.

The three women watched Janet pay the bill with an American credit card, give the waiter a too large tip in American money and they left. As they were doing so, Carleen thought to give them a slight tour of Windsor, Ontario, Canada, on the way home so there would be time for all of them to gather their wits and, how did Joe say it... "expand the story line" to whatever it was to be. And, she knew that the tour would please these two American girls. So she took them to the down river necking spot with a marvelous view of the two bridges that connected Canada with the States.

When they got back to Carleen's and had thanked her for the tour, they sat down in the living room, clearly with a hope that the new idea of how to continue to draw a map to the end of the Last Chapter would expand — but how, and how long that might take... time was indeed running out, worried Janet.

When they had settled Carleen said, "I am pleased that you can be patient with me and this, and I hope Joe doesn't walk in here in the midst of all this and wonder if I, the woman who says she loves him and respects his work — is now considering extending a pass at the unthinkable."

Janet nodded at this, but she kept still waiting to see what might be said next. Hanna jumped in, "I think this is amazing, and I don't know what you have in mind, Carleen, but here you are. And, if I am reading Jannie's face right, maybe you have a new thought of the way to expand your vision — we can call it a vision, and then how to turn the dilemma into success." She smiled, "...and maybe Joe will return and see you in a new light... all writers yearn for a, I don't know, Jannie, what do they call them...?"

"Spirit Guides."

" I hope that's you, Carleen, a Spirit Guide."

"I am going to suggest to you that even Spirits need help, assistants expanding ideas... I don't know this minute what might be an idea to expand The Chapter, all I understand is that I don't know what the components should be and I need some help!" She looked at Janet, "I understand that time is something you are out of, but if you could give me some of that time you don't have to stop and quietly think about this. We, working together, might be able to come up with something."

She paused to let the girls take that in.

Hanna looked at Janet. Janet said, "...well, I don't think any of us have faced the "transformation" issue... someone has to be transformed and my guess is the best candidate for that is Hollis."

It was Carleen, "... I think that's right, it appears to me that we haven't looked back and examined the meaning of her past which seems, so far in the story, kind of nonexistent, and where we might take that. My thought is to examine the possibilities her past and see what emerges. How does that sound?"

Hanna thought to herself as if Carleen had been at the Inn of Storms last night, about 2500 miles from where they were sitting right now, and she had watched them at dinner at the Inn of Storms. Beyond that, she had actually seen the girl who had told the Dead Art Dealer that she would not sleep with him, but now, with the possibility of this new fellow character, would that girl be ready to roll in the hay, dance on the sand, and neck with him on Brain Island...? And what else in the world could happen here if they were willing to explore in that direction?

"As I was saying, it appears to me that I have a-sort-of-handle on what Joe might have had in mind... And it seems to be the other side of what happened in the first non-sexy scene in the book... that is, where Hollis, the girl, says she won't sleep with him, the waves are crashing outside the window, the dealer is, what, several miles past Disappointed and so on and so on... My thought, now that we have a new man, is that the first part of this Chapter should be taken up with the new romance of the man and Hollis until we come to a new character determination and that could point to a resolve." She paused to let the two woman take that in...

It was Hanna, "...and then we can go on to wrapping up the story and the people and the chapter to make the publishers happy and probably make Joe very, very angry with Carleen here — are we worried about that?"

Janet and Carleen stared at her as if they had seen the Ghost of Charles Dickens (or Danielle Steele) Past. But each of them nodded at her as if they understood, but then, they hadn't asked Hanna if she had any ideas. Maybe she did... she read books, didn't she... maybe the point of view of a reader would be helpful here.

Suddenly, Carleen shouted out... "Yes, and wait, I think we have missed something... That something was a bit of a puzzle when it first came up in the story. Do you remember that, Janet?"

"You are speaking of Hollis, right?"

"Yes, Hollis and the beginning with her and Kinkaid arranging to leave New York and come here. There was all that business with getting Hollis some new clothes, and more important, working out how they would BE together at the Inn of Storms — an idea that Kinkaid chose to ignore in the marvelous scene Joe wrote about how Hollis wouldn't sleep with Hugh Kinkaid."

Hanna said, "I think it would be fun to write the flip side of that scene with Hollis and our new guy."

The other two nodded and smiled… wonder what that might be like?

Then Carleen piped in, "I think we have passed up something important and that maybe even Joe missed it." Carleen seemed to pause as if to bite her tongue.

"What do you mean?" asked Janet.

Carleen said, "I wonder if there isn't a detail that at the time didn't seem important, and maybe we didn't even understand it, so we glided by it in the story… but," and she paused here to catch her own breath, "on the way to the airport in New York, Kinkaid and his new girl, Hollis, are in the back of the taxicab — Hugh asks the driver to stop at a bank and he gets out, saying he will be right back. He goes into the bank, gets the notary public there — they all have them — to certify his signature on a piece of paper that if anything should happen to him, the art dealer, Hugh Kincaid, that Hollis Warfield will be asked to work at or take over his Gallery."

Carleen paused for effect, "Now we all glazed over that as unimportant, assuming, I guess, that Hollis made Kinkaid 'promise her something' and this is what Kinkaid did as a, what shall we call it, a sham idea to offer her nothing, but make it seem like SOMEthing" she paused here, "but what if— now that Kinkaid has accidently died, what if Hollis stepped forward to 'honor that agreement' and went back to NY to do just that. Might that be the kind of transformation Joe Kellnur was looking for, and we don't know if he missed his own idea there or not?"

There was a silence in the room that seemed palpable. The three women sat there in the comfort of this well-decorated living room, facing a woman whose face showed as much determination as Helene must have had at Troy… many minutes went by before anyone spoke.

Finally, it was Hanna and Janet at the same time… Hanna smiled at Jannie and nodded for her to continue…

"It's a simple question that's hard to answer, Carleen. You have been amazing in your patience and understanding of all this, and yes, we know you are doing it for love." She paused here, then, "Would you like us to stay and work together with you on this, your generous offer to write this last chapter — as well as determine how 'transformation' will work here?" She smiled here, "You might want to go to your library and look up the various definitions of 'ghostwriter.'" Jannie smiled at her interior thought of Joe Kellnur as ghostwriter and the book he had written for the woman in Denver. She said nothing and waited.

"I would like to think on this, thinking like Joe, to see if I could pull this together. Could you give me a few days of that time you don't have to give?"

Janet smiled at her, "You bet we can." She continued, "It's a most reasonable thought, and I am grateful that one who knows Joe and his work so well from the inside out is willing to think more on this. So yes, we can…" she looked at Hanna, "we can go somewhere and wait…"

Carleen gave her a grateful look and said, "Don't know if you do this, but there's a casino on this side of the river — might want to try it out. It's fun if you don't take it seriously, Joe takes me there occasionally… and it's a Hotel-Resort so you could stay there until I give you a call. How does that sound?"

The girls looked at each other, Hanna smiled. Finally Janet said, "…well, why not… you have a better chance at this than we do, and I'd rather try giving you time before trying to find him in the worlds of Shakespeare or Shaw."

Carleen smiled. "Thanks… I will be serious about this… I will."

In the car driving off, each of them had the same two thoughts at the same moment — first one, driving off from Colleen's place: "WHAT'S going ON HERE?" and then the second: trying to find where they were in Windsor: "WHAT is THIS doing here?" The last thing they expected to see in Canada was a casino, even though Colleen had said it was here — and, later they would find there was also one in Niagara Falls, maybe even three or four, but here in this quiet corner of Canada? Well, it said CASINO CANADA right on the front with all the lights. Let's go in.

After the quiet life they had been living with the Mysteries of JK, the lovely drive across Michigan, the sedateness of Carleen's home, it felt like they had walked into a circus, or at least driven to Las Vegas.

"What shall we do?" It was Janet, looking at the array of gaming tables.

"What do you like to do, besides play bridge, which they don't do here."

"Gin rummy?"

"Well, if they do that here sounds boring... hey, Girl, aren't you attracted to the roll of the dice and the whirl of the wheel?"

"Yes, yes, the Whirl-of-the-Wheel-in-Windsor."

They walked around until they could agree on which Wheel and finally settled at a table off to the side. There were two other people, an older couple, the sort of folks you wouldn't have expected to be here. But, there was a good sized pile of chips in front of them. "Whoops, chips," said Hanna and she grabbed Jannie's purse and ran off to the cashier.

Jannie sat and watched the old couple rake it in. She couldn't tell if they had a "system" or not... but they seemed to go back and forth between odds and evens and blacks and reds. It made Janet dizzy, but Hanna came back and Janet put a hand on hers and semi-pointed to the old couple, as if to say "watch them."

The two friends watched and watched and Janet grew more and more confused, but finally Hanna nodded and put some chips on the table and smiled at the croupier. He smiled back and spun the wheel. This time the old couple lost and Hanna won. Janet was stunned, she leaned over and whispered in Hanna's ear... "How did you do THAT..." Hanna merely looked askance at her and nodded her head.

The old couple were now watching the girls, but continued to play their "pattern" of odd numbers and reds. Hanna laid down chips on the table. the dealer gave her an odd look and spun the wheel.

Hanna won again and the old couple lost. Very quickly the woman picked up their chips, grabbed her husband by the arm and left the table. The dealer seemed pleased with that until he turned back to Hanna, who gestured for him to spin-the-wheel-mister.

It seemed to take the wheel longer to spin and slow down, but when it did, Hanna was a winner again. In three rolls she had amassed a considerable pile. She smiled at Jannie, "...fun, huh..." Jannie smiled, yes, and Hanna raked up their chips and said, "I'm starved, let's eat..."

Suddenly the dealer was empty-handed, so he pulled out a deck of cards and began to play solitaire, watching the two woman stroll off. He shook his head, as if to acknowledge his own strange job.

They strolled around the casino, until Jannie saw the dining room and turned them in that direction. Hanna looked at Jannie smiling, "Fun, fun, fun, eh... and as I am here with you about to have yet another Canadian meal, I have a vision of a different kind of meal, there is a small pile of red chips on your left breast and a small pile of black chips on your right breast and my thought is to see how long it will take me to lick them off..." Janet smiled and was about to say...

"What will it be for you lovely ladies, and Welcome to Casino Canada. I'll bet you are American...?" said the waiter in his best Canadian accent.

While they were waiting for dinner, Hanna said, "How do you suppose she is doing... think we should stop over in the morning and check in with her?"

Jannie continued Hanna's unspoken thought, "...or should we go watch some Shakespeare?"

"My thought is to give her a few days to work through this... all the while knowing that she is hoping that Joe will come right in through her front door and that he won't throw any dish ware at her, but will sit down beside her and help her, help him — God, what a relief..."

Janet was not as certain, "...but try to remember I am with a publisher who expects me to say that either I found the Last Chapter or I found Joe Kellnur who handed it to me… How can I explain to them that SHE wrote the Last Chapter?"

"Easy, Jannie," said Hanna, putting her hand on Janet's. "Listen, I did some internet research and this is my thought: The Stratford Shakespeare Festival is now playing six plays continually along that lovely River Pond they have. We can drive there in about an hour and a half, see some plays, shop at their marvelous book stores and have a picnic lunch on that cute little island by the theater. Do this for two or three days and come back and see that Joe has not come back and laid waste to Carleen and is waiting in the kitchen to do us in…" Hanna smiled at her own joke and poked Jannie in the ribs.

It was one of those moments with Janet that she felt blessed to have a good friend who was sensible — even one who had a sense of the world and was trying her best to look out for her friend.

"Hey, Sweetie, think of it this way, we can have a free paid vacation watching Shakespeare and shopping in Stratford… all the while knowing that Carleen, who knows the author best, and is inside the story, is working-on-IT."

It was only a few seconds before Janet said, "Oh why not… this is the first really reasonable idea I have heard —faced in some long time." Hanna smiled and Jannie looked off in the distance.

Hanna said, still holding Jannie's hand, "I'll bet this isn't the end of the world, Sweetie, and isn't it lucky that we are doing this on the company's Expense Account."

Jannie, trying to be serious, said, "Even More Marvelous."

"And, I know this will sound dumb, and actually, I hate to admit it, but I have never seen a play by Shakespeare…what are they like?"

Jannie was stunned, here was her smart friend who had never… oh my, what to say? "Well, it's Grand, that's the only word that comes to mind…Grand. The language is of a long, long time ago, and you need to get used to that, but if you think of the play as A Story, they are pretty marvelous, I mean...*Romeo and Juliet... Hamlet... As You Like it...* and a play they don't do often is *Coriolanus*. It's one of my favorites... quite amazing."

Then, Janet thought for a moment... "...you know they have made movies of his plays. You've never seen one of those?"

"Aaaaahhh, yes, now that you mention it... Richard and his lady Elizabeth Taylor."

"Oh, sure they were good at that." She thought for a moment, "Wellthen, we need to get started, let's check out of the hotel and get a map that can help us arrive in Stratford, Ontario..."

Work-In-Progress
"the last chapter"

Carleen had to smile at what was in front of her... she had been deeply bent over her computer, thinking, thinking, thinking about the scene in Joe's book where the Art Dealer man was in the hotel room with the girl who was taking her clothes off to show him "what he was not going to have." Only Joe could write a scene like that. Carleen wanted to do that same scene with her new man character, but with a twist... how to do that? ...and now it was here in front of her, she had written it. This time she had truly amazed herself, yet at the same time knowing that if Joe had not written "his scene" she could not have written "her scene"...well, it was going in the novel now.

She read it again...

They had spent a day walking around the Inn of Storms, and its beach as if getting to know the place instead of each other.

The long walks on the beach were fun, too... plus watching the Artist Man set up to do "paintings" of Brain Island. The best part was watching him try to "walk around the small island." He thought all the water would be shallow until he walked into a drop-off bank and was six feet under. Fortunately, his wife had come that day and she fished him out and helped him catch his floating-away-paints. What a laugh.Now, on this shady afternoon, the couple found themselves back at the Inn and in her room. Hollis looked at him against the light of the window and felt a yearning. She took off her light jacket, she kicked off her shoes, and still watching his back, decided that she really did yearn for him... up close, laying down, eye to eye. As George turned around, he was surprised to see Hollis almost fully unclothed. He seemed to need steadying, so he reached for a chair and by the time he had steadied himself and come to realize what was happening, or what would happen, he was stunned.

She smiled at him. He smiled at her. Almost involuntarily, he said, "My, you are a lovely, lovely woman... but, ah, what are you planning to do?" As soon as he said it, he realized how stupid that was... what was she planning to do?

He rushed over to her just as her slip fell to the floor. He gave her a big hug and a light kiss. As he held her, he said into her ear, softly..."Listen, I think you are a marvelous woman and I have loved our time together, and yes, how could I not have thoughts about you this way..." here he stepped back a little to look at her before pulling her close again... "but don't you think it's too soon for us to do this... shouldn't we get to know each other a bit more..." he looked at her closely, "...ah, no, you don't... of course, what a dummy I am. Listen, can we sit on the bed for a moment and talk about this, about how this would be a wonderful thing to do when we know each other better... inside out, as it were... Please, let's think on this." That said, he leaned back, pulling her with him and reached for a blanket to cover her... and him. "Yes, let's think on this... you are special, you know, and I am scared..."

Carleen leaned back and looked at the scene... her scene, and thought, "I'll bet Joe would think this... ah, child's-play... what! They don't make love right away? But no, I like this better..." and then she smiled to herself and realized that she had written the EX-act opposite scene from what-Joe-would-write. She smiled. He is off somewhere in Canada looking for his inspiration and I am right here. She had tried to convince him that SHE was his inspiration, but that had failed... no, she realized, it wasn't her, it was some "writer's idea" in his head that he needed something else... Carleen had not thought of that before, that he might need "something else"— now there was a thought worth some deep consideration.

Carleen paused to get up and walk around all the rooms of her house on the main floor. She needed an idea, an instant... she sensed that she didn't have much time — in real time — nor much time in this Last Chapter to accomplish the transformation of Hollis... well, how about a... how would Joe say it...a brief prelude.

I'll bet that was what was haunting Joe and she had to face it too... but now she was alone and had to face the assignment herself, all by herself ...

...well all right, what has happened to Change Hollis?

She failed with Hugh Kincaid

She failed with George Spelvin

...both good men

...so now let's get serious here: they were leaving to go back to New York in a day or so... Hollis had the piece of paper Hugh had given her... She had George's offer to get to know him better... How could she do that, she didn't even know herself better. Maybe it was time to quit with men for awhile, try to learn something from this about herself and move, move, move — she wasn't used to thinking like that, but now she could not only think about something but now she could ACTUALLY DO SOMETHING. Oh my God — I'm not used to this, this has never happened before.

Yes, she had screwed up with Hugh Kincaid, yes, George was delicious but he was a Canadian, and yes, she was delicious but she was an American woman who needed an amazing opportunity — there were men everywhere, let's not worry about that!

However, no matter how delicious she was, she was an American who needed an amazing opportunity. Could it be right in front of her NOW?

Carleen had walked in and out of every room in her home and was now at the back door, facing the yard and the table setting there. She looked at her watch and thought… must be time for dinner. Surely there was a"writer's rule" that a snack or even a good meal would incite the imagination cells in the writer's head. Fine, let's eat. Or wait, maybe she needed a walk along the river… not eat, but think…

"Well, what did you think of THAT?" said Hanna.

"Even though I live in New York, I am not a playgoer. Just seeing this production of *Midsummer's Night Dream* makes me wonder if I haven't made a big mistake that needs to be re-thought…why not begin to go to the theater more?"

Hanna nodded.

"The part I liked the best was the workmen doing that play for the Royals… cute and fun." She looked at Hanna, "Let me guess the part that you liked the best. That lovely scene in the woods where the lovers meet and, don't you love this word from the past — 'declaim' their love for each other. What's good about this play is the odd mix of fun and love and how they intertwine together."

Hanna kept nodding. What she admired about her friend Jannie, was that she was so smart… but she decided to keep quiet and have another bite of her left-over sandwich on the Island — how she loved this Island-in-the-Pond right beside the theatre. Interrupting that thought was that they had decided they should probably go back to Windsor tomorrow and see how Carleen was doing. Oh my… what would the world say if they found out the author's girlfriend wrote the last chapter of his book? She couldn't get over the odd amazement of this thought. Oh, well…

Fortunately Janet had her cell phone and she could call New York and make up some outrageous story about how she had a new idea of where That Last Chapter Is… and that she was going to pursue that line of inquiry and report back. No, no, she didn't have the time now to go into details, but this New Pursuit was hopeful and she would get-back-to-them. Yes, she would, because it occurred to Janet that if this crazy idea didn't work out, she would be out of a job. Well, Hanna would love that, because then she, Hanna, could talk Jannie into moving in with her and writing Her Own Novel... oh, my...

Carleen leaned back from her, what was that Joe used to say...
ghostwriting
as "her chapter" continued:

Hollis was on her way down the steps of the Inn to the beach when Kerry Cox hailed her and she joined him below.

"Hi Hollis, any chance you can come over to The Island with me?"

"Sure, Kerry... you mean now?"

"Yep."

She got to the bottom of the steps and fell in with him across the wide beach to the "entrance" to what they had been calling Brain Island. Hollis had not been there but had heard all the jokes about it, but to Kerry it seemed most interesting and he was serious. He was convinced that THIS island with its peculiarities would be the inspiration for his next body of work.

Once on the island, Hollis was surprised that Kerry's wife had organized a reasonably comfortable setting for people to sit and be together... though Hollis was sure not many people had come... it was, after all, a strange place...tunnels and all ... well, it felt like being inside someone's brain... pretty unique, she thought.

"Quite a place, eh? We love it here and I'll show you around in a minute, 'cause there is a place on the far side where you can sit in comfort and watch the tides and the sunset."

"Well thanks, Kerry, say, where is your wife?"

"She's on the way, bringing a picnic to have later, you can stay if you want, there's always enough."

Hollis smiled. Kerry looked at her in a deep way. "Some odd things going on lately... I think we are getting over the loss of Hugh, but on the other hand, we are pretty anxious about what happens next with the gallery. Hugh said you had shown an interest in it —"

Hollis smiled, "Why yes, art has always been an interest for me, I have just never had the chance to — what, get into it, I guess. But, Hugh and I talked about it a lot."

"Uh huh... yes, you have any background in it?"

"Well, yes and no, I guess. I dated a guy in New York who worked in a gallery and he was always telling me things and he even took me to his gallery once, when no one was there and kind of, you know, got serious about what he wanted to do to bring in more people and get some sales, even in a tough... what did he call it... a tough art market? Yes, that sounds right."

"We are all going home tomorrow and Alice and I were wondering if you would spend some time with us in the gallery now that Hugh is gone... we, ah, we think what happened between you and Hugh may have rubbed off on you and..."

"Listen, Kerry, I don't think Hugh mentioned this to you, and no one really knows but me and him, and now that he's gone, we miss him. He was a sweet guy, but back in the room, I have his things, and there are some papers he had made before we left New York that... gee, I don't know how to say this, but give me the right to have, to work at, to... ah maybe the way to say it is... the right for me to take care of the gallery in case anything happened to him." She watched Kerry for a reaction and then said... "I know this is kind of odd, but it goes with what you were just saying... that is, maybe we could do things together at the gallery..." and here she gestured around her, "...'cause you are going to have some new paintings soon, right."

Kerry shook his head, seemingly in wonder. "Hollis, I think

that you and I and Alice are going to have an interesting time to-gether... and I think you are the one who can pull this together... want to do it together?" He didn't wait for an answer. "I know lots of things must be going through your mind right now... it's been a chaotic time in a place that was supposed to give us some rest... and I don't mean to ask questions that are too personal, but do you have any plans with George Spelvin?"

"Nope, I don't... he's a nice fellow and all that, but what you are saying here to me has a lot of meaning... hopefully for you, surely for me, and maybe together we can do as well at this as Hugh Kin-caid did... What do you think?"

"I knew it... I told Alice this was the kind of woman you were. She'll be here soon and we will tell her this good news together." He got up off the rock he was sitting on and walked over to Hollis and gave her a hug.

"Thanks, Hollis, thanks so much, good luck to us all.

Joe had always said to Carleen, "Always take a look at what has come out of the typewriter (he always called his computer that) to see what it says..." She had been at it for a full day now, no lunch, no nap, no nothing but seeming to pour herself out into the story. That's always what Joe said, so if she was going to be him for a while, that's what she would do: pour and pour some more.

Carleen wasn't sure what she was pouring but on the other hand, she had something and felt like the cup needed a refill, so I guess, why not pour-some-more... fingers crossed...

Hollis Kieffer sat in the art gallery office and read the morning Times as if in a daze. She had never read about herself in the newspa-per and she read avidly to see how the story — her life? — came out. Yet there was an intelligence to the manner in which she read about herself, perhaps in levels, as if she knew how her life had come out but that perhaps the reporter could bring it to another, yet unknown place. The sunlight through the window seemed to move across the newsprint, illuminating and shadowing in the same swift movement. The sun, a swift element...

Yes. The reporter brought her young life thus far to an unfamiliar place. He had glossed over the farm life. He had, true to the ethic of new journalism, now called in-depth reporting, penetrated deep into her street life and made a lyrical transition to her present station in life. He is writing his own poetry, not hers. Much like a film reviewer will be so enthusiastic about the movie that he will want to be the screen writer and thus wax, not critically insightful, but dance to his own scene in the movie — often binding himself to the wrong angle of the story — the one that magnetizes him.

"Miss Keiffer, Mr. Cox is at the back entrance with a truck. Thought you'd like to know."

Hollis nodded and looked back at the newspaper.

The phone rang. "Hollis, it's for you."

"Yes, yes," Hollis said on the phone, nodding and listening, distracted. "Oh, well I just read it myself, Mr. Keats." More nodding. "Yes, quite a surprise. Well, I'm sorry you feel that way... yes, I understand... of course..."

Nodding and more nodding, "What do I think? Well, I'm only sorry that the reporter guy didn't do more background... I mean more about my growing up on a farm in Connecticut, that I was a good girl until I was 17 and fell off the wagon... no, bad word, I was not an alcoholic, — just a "bad girl," well, until Hugh Kincaid rehabilitated me, you know, he had a talent for sniffing out what can be saved or made right in a person — I miss him every day of my life, but he is gone, and I am here, and I think you are still here, too,

Mr. Keats, even though you now want to buy your art elsewhere. I know Hugh would be disappointed. Whoops, sorry to interrupt, but one of the artists is at the back door with something delicious, and I must…"

With not very much nodding nor listening, Hollis said, "Nope, I can't tell you. I promised not to say who it was or when we would be showing this new piece, but if Hugh was here, he would say it was 'a hot one.' 'Bye, Mr. Keats."

Hollis walked quickly to the back of the gallery, through the storage area and onto the dock.

"Hi, Kerry. Looks like you have an even bigger one for me this time."

They hug briefly and Kerry kisses her on the cheek as if she were his little sister. "Yep, I'm afraid it is Hollis, will that be all right?"

As Kerry is opening the back of the van, Joseph Willard comes onto the dock. He nods at Kerry, who says, "Hi, Willard…" and turns to Hollis.

"Could I have a word?" He pulls her off of the dock.

"Hollis, I know Kerry called yesterday to say he was coming and that he had a large piece. But, Hollis, we just can't…"

She braced herself, as if for a beating. She had not gotten over men speaking loud in her face and trying to be polite about it. What was wrong with these folks, anyway? I have told them and then told them again, can't they hear? "I appreciate your concern, Joseph," her words soothing him, calling him Joseph, almost stroking him as if he were a John. "We are going to make space for Kerry Cox until someone comes in here and makes me a decent offer for this Place…"

This Place, in her phrasing, was the definition of ambivalence. She looked levelly at him and waited for what he would say next, which would be some variation of "space."

"Listen, the Catullus show is coming in and she has long pieces that will need some air around them... I have already made a hanging plan for her show which I can show you — and the plan calls for moving Kerry Cox elsewhere... and I have determined that as well, but there is no space for a big, new Kerry Cox with this incoming show... Hollis."

She patted his arm and turned to see if Kerry could hear.

"I'm sorry, Joseph, but I want this piece up for the opening of Catullus. You can take the others down if you need, but this one —"

"—you haven't even seen this one, and if I can be this bold, neither have I... Hollis we can't run a gallery this way."

"We are, and you have done a marvelous job, Joseph...this is not the end of the world." She leaned away from him as if to play a key card. "I have seen the end of the world and it doesn't look anything like this."

A stage pause.

"OK?"

"All right."

Joseph Willard turns and leaves. Kerry sticks his head out of the van and says, "Isn't he going to see what I have here?"

"Not to worry, Kerry, he has stuff to do. I want to see what you have been doing."

Kerry pulled the piece out of the van and leaned it against the dock wall. He pulled her off to the side as if he was going to reveal the last secret.

"Did you read the Times yet?"

She slapped him on the arm. "Yes, yes, I read the Times, what else is there to do? And I see that my — what is that word my mother used to use — lurid past has been splashed all over New York. A shamed woman, that was my father's line. Fuck it, Kerry, I am going to cut it out and send it over to the framer for a big expensive gold frame and hang it in the window so everyone can see. What an idea. The artists will love it and the collectors, Mr. Keats has already been heard from, will hate it. and, I plan to stand between them and laugh… laugh pretty loud…"

The New York Times   November 17, 2016

Hollis Kieffer at the Kincaid Gallery

In the traditional manner of gallery protocol the headline would read, Kerry Cox at the Kincaid Gallery. That is, this artist is at this gallery. It's the way of that world. And, just to note, Kerry Cox is at the Kincaid Gallery, and at least according to Joseph Willard, the current Gallery Director, Kerry Cox should not be at the Kincaid Gallery. So the mystery doubles and is surrounded by the question of why these people are at the Kincaid Gallery and who is manning the Ship. Willard claims it is not he.

Included in the mystery is the unexpected and violent death of the former gallery owner, Hugh Kincaid. He and Ms. Kieffer, with Kerry Cox and his wife, were together on the West Coast of Vancouver Island to watch the great Pacific Storms is the spoken reason for their being there together. During a mighty storm, Mr. Kincaid was lost into the storm and no amount of searching could find his body.

On their return to New York, it is learned that on the day of leaving for Canada, Hugh Kincaid signed a paper giving Ms. Kieffer ownership of the gallery in case of his death or incapacity. Further investigation reveals that Kincaid and Kieffer had known each other for barely two weeks before departing on this intimate, we assume, trip and intimate, we know, agreement. John Grisham, where are you when we need you?

Well, we know who is Kerry Cox, an artist that was discovered and promoted by Kincaid. A successful show was held only last month. But, who is Hollis Kieffer? No record of her at lesser positions with other galleries or museums. No record of her educational accomplishments at good curatorial schools. Nothing at The Rhode Island School of Design or the California Art Clutter Places. Where did Ms. Kieffer gain the credability to become the director of one of Chelsea's more prominent contemporary art galleries? (In all fairness to Ms. Kieffer, it should be noted that her first dabble at the gallery was to hire Joseph Willard, a well-known New York gallery director.)

So about her, who would think to look into the files at Covenant House, the largest shelter for runaway teenagers in the world at the corner of 42nd and Broadway? Who would think to look into the police files at Manhattan Central — District 31? These are not usually the breeding grounds for up and coming art dealers. Yet these are surely Hollis Kieffer's roots and qualifications, as known primarily by Hugh Kincaid.

When asked, Joseph Willard only shrugs and says "I am an art dealer."

Well. I am not John Grisham, so I can't tell you what the dead know, or pierce the heart of this deep mystery, or assemble the clues in a meaningful way. I can only report the facts as they present themselves:

1. Ms. Hollis Kieffer has a police record as long as your arm for vagrancy, petty theft and prostitution.

2. Ms. Hollis Kieffer was in the care of Covenant House on and off for several years, her first appearance being in March three years ago.

3. Little is known of her family, but she claimed to the authorities to be from a farm in the northwest most portion of Connecticut. It should be noted here that runaway kids will not tell you where they are from or their real name, for obvious reasons — don't want to be shipped home. Finally,

4. She met Hugh Kincaid at a party in SoHo 13 days before they

left together for Kennedy Airport to travel to Seattle together for a "vacation" and, according to sources quoting Kincaid, "...a thinking/planning trip..." Kincaid was well known for bringing a new level of thinking, planning, marketing, promotion and high profile salesmanship to the new contemporary art scene. Being a former stock broker, such was the way his (art) mind worked.

I don't want to cast any aspersions on the way Ms. Kieffer's mind might work, moving from her former occupation to the new contemporary art scene. We can only assume a new body of thinking will emerge, hopefully one that will continue to enlighten the art world in lower Manhattan.

Hollis looks up from the paper just as Joseph knocks lightly at the door to her office. "Can you come to see, please."

Joseph has carefully found the deepest recess in the gallery space and hung Kerry Cox's new piece, entitled

My Mind: Untangling the Tangle

...in a place where it can be seen, but not enough space to just stand back and admire it.

"OK?"

"Fine, Joseph. Thank you."

There is a moment between them. Hollis braces herself for what will be another pleading for order and business and sales and....

"I want to thank you, Hollis," he said.

"For what?"

"The piece in the *Times* today. It's good news that will do us well."

Carleen leaned back with an odd sensation:

…it was done

…she had finished

…oh, I hope, I hope.

The Last Chapter is Here!

The Celebration Dinner came immediately after the three of them had stopped at Fed Ex and sent off an overnight letter to Jonas K on Sixth Avenue in New York, New York. It was Carleen's Last Chapter. They loved it, wanted to read it again, and been excited to send it off to the Publisher, that is, Janet's boss. She was off the hook and could look forward to a suitable reward and an elaborate "thank you" for a job of Literary Detection well done. The gossip columnists (if they ever found out about it) would surely call this caper a Smash.

The three attractive women, dressed to the Nines had the corner table at Canada Star, the finest restaurant on the River Rouge. They had a long and loud dinner in which two of the women had constantly raised their glasses to the third woman and made a toast. The words seemed to revolve around "...the best woman Ghost Writer/Lover in the World, forget about Canada and the U S of A..."

...and so it went until they surely had enough wine. Then home. Carleen wanted them to stay in the Guest Room which was prepared and they all fell into bed, fully saturated with novel pages and wine.

In the morning, Jannie and Hanna got up and dressed for home. Light breakfast, lots of smiles and hugs and promises to be together again...and they left. Hanna and Janet across the border to Metropolitan Airport west of Detroit and on the plane with her budging briefcase and an extra copy of the Last Chapter in case the Fed Ex plane crashed in Pennsylvania. Now, she would read that Last Chapter again on the plane to New York's La Guardia Airport.

Carleen went back home after stopping for some fruit for lunch at the market. Then, a quiet afternoon in her backyard. Carleen was ready for that, really ready. She suddenly felt exhausted. The stress the strain the pressure to finish the Last Chapter had been exciting and amazing and surprising and exhausting and,

and…

…and now, she could rest in the shade of her lovely trees. She was settled there when she heard steps up the side of the house, and the gate open. But, it was only the mailman, she thought, who was always considerate enough to bring special envelopes back to her.

She felt arms around her. OMG this can't be the mail man!

"Joe, ah… Darling… you're back… oh…"

And there he stood, smiling down at her, this missing, handsome American writer, now back from the writing grave… looking at her, his ghostwriter… Whoops, got to stop thinking like that.

"Joe, Darling, how good to see you, I have been so worried… wish you had called or something so I could have known for certain you were all right. Ah, are you all right?"

Joe Kellnur reaches into the case he has at his side and pulls out a clipped together, slim stack of pages. He hands them to her with a big smile…

"… you were right, Honey, Canada is filled with inspiration, aside from you, of course, I went all the way to the Shaw Festival in Niagara-on-the-Lake… what a spot that is… I would go see a play in the afternoon, then sit in that great park overlooking the lake. In the distance would be Toronto on a clear day… and I would think and make notes and finally, Damn it All, I Got It." He points to the papers in her hand… "There it is, and you will be the first to read it. I can't wait to hear what you think of it, My Last Chapter… forget what Jonas and his bunch think of it, it works, but I want to know what you think of it, you are My Muse."

Carleen looked at him as if he was the Greek God of Endings who came down on a God's Platform as the *Deus Ex Machina* to take care of the ending of This Play. Ohh My Godddd…

"…and now that I have finished it, Sweetheart…" he waved his copy of the Chapter at her… "then all we have to decide is what will be the first thing… well, first things first, a lovely roll in the sack with you and then a celebration dinner at that fancy place you like on the river —"

That said, Joe swooped down and scooped her up in his arms, giving her a light kiss. Then, through the double doors to her bedroom, where, still holding her, he tossed the copy of the Last Chapter, as if it were a pile of confetti, all over her bed. He kissed her again, and said, "…this Chapter is for you and I to celebrate the finish of the book and YOU… my inspiring Goddess," and with that, he laid her down on the Confetti Bed and rolled in alongside her.

Carleen had never thought it was possible to be enchanted and terrified at the same moment… here was the man she loved, right beside her, but under her was the crushed, crunched proof that she had betrayed him deeply. As he turned to put his arms around her, she burst into tears.

"What…what, Darling, what's wrong… Did I hurt you putting you down on the bed?" She shakes her head, No…

"…are you concerned we are about to imprint the Last Chapter with our steamy love? I have another copy in the car."

Carleen shakes her head, No…

A very long stage wait, and then she said: "I have done something un-thinkable, Joe, and I don't see how you will be able to forgive me… and I do love you, and you love me and…"

"…and, but what…?" he said.

"Oh, Joe, it's such a long and convoluted story, but the last of it was this very morning, when I and a woman from your publishing company sent your Last Chapter off Fed Ex to Jonas whatever-his-name is."

"You … how could…what…?"

"See what I mean… un-thinkable… but, Joe, I ah, ohhhhhh…" And, she turned over in another wail of tears.

It was as if he had become, right beside her, a marble statue of Charles Dickens, right there in her own bed in Windsor ,Ontario. Between them nothing moved, and she wasn't certain she was still breathing. Carleen reached over to touch him. He felt cold.

They lay there, in some sort of Chapterless Neverland for what seemed like hours… but was only minutes… maybe…

… then she said to him: "Joe, Joe, listen, it's me, Carleen. I love you so much, I would be willing to throw myself off the Windsor Bridge… and so, when this woman from your publishing company turned up on my doorstep wanting to know where-you-were… where-was-the-Last Chapter… and some other questions I didn't know the answers to… I was confused, already worried about you off somewhere, lost without your Chapter, somewhere in Canada. They, ah, there was a woman with her, they kept after me about Jonas, deadlines and how-to-find-a-last chapter… they were here for days… and finally, Oh God, Joe — I wrote a Last Chapter for YOUR BOOK. They liked it and they sent it to New York.

Oooooohhhhhhhhhhhhh what a nightmare… and now you are back here with me, we should both be glad and loving and joined in every possible way two people who love each other can be… and THIS is where WE ARE…. Ohhhhh, God, Joe what are we going to do? Joe, will you forgive me?"

Joe looked like the remains of a literary beating by the three Goddesses of Words and Chapters and, oh, yes, Jonas Keppleman, let's not forget him…

Carleen put her hand on the side of his head, and pulled him three inches closer and kissed him lightly. "Joe, Darling, I did this for you… try to remember that…actually, when you think about it, so did Janet Kidder and… oh, what does it matter…it's done…"

"Could I read it?"

"Read what?"

"The Last Chapter you wrote for me."

Carleen teared again until he put his arms around her. He pulled off enough of her clothes to roll over to her and begin to make love to her. "I don't care," he said, "what matters the most is what you have done for me and what we are to each other…"

She looked at him, his face was merged with her own, they had become one person, right then and there… I don't think he knows yet that the only reason I could write his Chapter for him is that we are one spirit and it doesn't matter if he is at one end of Ontario and I am at the other… we are writing the same last chapter at the same time, just as we are now, him within me and me within him… lovers and writers… Oh, that would be a good title for the Next Book.

Carleen squeezed him tightly, rose up into him as he lowered into her…

and they became a single body until an unholy scream was heard in her bedroom... and that's the last thing she remembered...

When morning light broke, Carleen opened her eyes and reached over to Joe... the bed was empty except for her. She sat up, disoriented... had he been here, or was that a dream... was he here and where... she got up, bare-assed, and looked out the window, no he wasn't there... she went to the kitchen and looked out that window to see him leaning over the bar-b-que grill... he was burning a sheaf of papers... Oh, no, don't, please don't... and as she thought it again, she heard herself saying it out the doorway to him.

Joe looked over and then down to her body. He smiled... "you are always especially lovely in the morning..." She was confused, but opened the backyard door and came out to him... not even remembering to look to see if the neighbors were in their yard watching the "show."

"What are you doing?" she said, as if he was pouring a cup of coffee for her breakfast.

"I, ah, felt the need for, what is the word, 'exorcism', yes, that's it, Exorcism."

"Exorcising what?"

"My Last Chapter."

"YOUR last chapter?"

"Yep, that's it."

"But, why?"

"You are some lovely woman... I have never seen you this way, in this morning light... beyond marvelous. Would the neighbors object if we lay down on the chaise there and loved a little?"

"I... ah, oh, Joe... but wait just a moment, what are you doing there?"

"Burning a Last Chapter — it's been so witchy and troublesome that I thought it best to burn it... you remember... Burn, Baby, Burn?"

"Joe, be serious for a moment... I..."

"I am being as serious as I can be, having a casual conversation with the most special woman in Canada, beckoning me with her stark, lovely body… why don't I leave this for later and we can go back inside," he turned to the chaise lounge behind him, "or would you rather make love to me there?"

She smiled and looked down again to see that she was, indeed, stark naked in her own backyard. She looked over to the chaise, and shook her head. She looked to the fencing around her home… no neighbors gaping and enjoying "the show."

Carleen took the three steps toward him, raising up her body and breasts to meet him and took his hand… "…will you make love to me this morning?"

"Yes, I will… I can burn this later…"

"What are you burning?"

"I told you, The Last Chapter of my book. The Exorcism"

Carleen dropped his hand and fell back onto the chaise. "What… ah, why are… why are you doing that?"

"Listen, Sweetheart, we have had a most trying time here… me with my God damned Last Chapter, you dealing with the New York Woman, me with trying to get Bernard Shaw to help me write… and now we have the unthinkable… two Last Chapters."

"Ah, Joe, Honey…"

" … so after coming back to life last night in your bed, and getting up with the morning sun and reading Your Last Chapter… I realized something very important…"

"What, Honey… what…?"

"Your Last Chapter is better than mine. Pure and simple."

"But how could…"

"My last Chapter is not as interesting nor as true-to-the-characters-in-the-story as yours… so, what we are trying to do here, ah… is write good books with fine stories and meaningful endings. I have written an all right book, and you, with your sensible sensitivity have understood what the right (character) ending would be… and have done it… all the while remembering that I wanted to write a Novel of Character… well, Honey, you nailed it."

He paused again and looked at her deeply, "Did you hear? Your last chapter is better than my last chapter and we can have only one last chapter in any one book."

He dropped down to his knees in front of her and looked up into her eyes, "Thank you, Goddess of Saved Last Chapters," and then sensing again that he was face to face with her lovely nude body, rose, taking her up and walked through the kitchen saying…

"After our little wake-me-up in your bedroom, I'll make you breakfast — I can make a good breakfast, you'll see…"

…and he walked them back into her bedroom flooded with morning sunlight.

ANNEX
Janet's Briefcase Contents

Braille
(the remainder of the story)

The room was small, it had to be because it was a cottage rather than a full blown house. The room was neat and well kept. Blasted with sunlight, it seemed a haven rather than a place — his strongest impression was of books. Books everywhere. A wall of them to his left over the fireplace and a bookcase of them along the back wall, beside the door to what he assumed to be the kitchen.

"Please feel free to look around. As you have already seen, I have nothing to hide. It's a very small house."

"You have a lot of books." He picked one out of the shelf and opened it. It was in braille. He ran his finger over the raised white dots. They had a pleasing sensation, he wondered what was the name of the book. "Yes, I love them," she said. She was standing a few feet from him.

" But you have been kind to be my rescuer — please let me make you some coffee. I make good coffee and this is a lucky day for both of us, because I made cinnamon coffee cake."

"Sure, that would be great. Can I, ah, help you?"

Aleta laughed and walked into the kitchen. "Please feel free to look around."

Todd found a tiny bedroom with barely enough room for a bed, but which had a large walk-in closet, a good sized bathroom and a door that lead out to a deck and a hot tub. There was a stack of books by the tub and another beside the bed.

He couldn't get over the isolation here, and just as he had that thought, music rose up through the house. It seemed to rise from the floors and fill the walls and was of such a tremor that it made him tremble for a moment until he accustomed himself to it.

"I like to have breakfast inside and listen out to the ocean."

...listen out to the ocean...

"... I can feel the warmth of the day, but I don't have to worry about sunburn on my skin... it's very sensitive... so in this room... " her voice came though the doorway toward him... "... I have the best of everything, the sound of Chopin, the voice of the ocean and the warmth of the sun. Will you come to join me." Her voice was warm and softer than before.

He came to the living room and sat across from her. She handed him, as if she were a sighted person, his cup of coffee without a waver in the surface of the black liquid along with a plate with what appeared to be the most delicious cinnamon cake he had ever seen. Todd shook himself slightly as if to come awake. Immediately she said, "Are you all right?"

"What do you mean... "

"... well, you seem at odds here. I understand this is an unusual situation and you may not be comfortable."

She was right. He was not. All this seemed so unreal to him. This beautiful woman living alone with only a dog in an isolated cove along the ocean. He looked closely at her, and he could because she could not see him boldly staring. She was a most beautiful woman and there was something... something else... .

"What is it like to be blind," she said.

"What... I beg your pardon?" Todd replied.

"What is it like to be blind," she said again. Todd looked at her and she was smiling. "... well... ?"

"How would I know that?" he said.

"Have you ever thought of what it might be like?"

"No."

"Stop to think a moment... I have never been sighted. I have only felt the sun... I have only touched flowers... I can know your face only with my fingers... I can never know how you look in your entirety, yet I can feel your fabrics and get a sense of them… but what colors look better on you is unknowable to me… yet my darkness is a comfort to me, my dog is my lover, I can "see" every bit of this place where I live because it is small and I have run my hand over every inch of it. I have held all the books and read many of them… it may seem that I read a lot, but they are only a comfortable presence to me… my sisters know that and each time they come they bring another one. Braille is a sensuous language. The language of touch. I love to touch things. I can know them by touching."

Another silence. "Do you like the dark?"

Todd thought for a moment, "I am not afraid of the dark."

"Good."

"Why?"

"I think that many people respond to my blindness because of their own fear of the dark, but if you do not fear the darkness, why then there is something else."

"Something else?"

"Something else that is on your mind about me."

"Well, now that you say it, yes," he wondered how she was so attuned to him, how she could know what he was thinking or about to ask. He had never had such an experience with a person. "Well, I just don't think it's safe for you to live in such an isolated place."

"You are worried about my safety. How kind. I wonder what else you are thinking about?"

"You make this sound as if it was a gift."

"Life is a gift and I have life. Other things, the language of smell and touch are all the ribbons and bows, special additions to the gift, including the choice of the giver. You have given me two gifts this morning."

"Two?"

She sensed the space between them and moved closer to

him. Then, she touched his face… first lightly over his eyelashes and then across his eye lids. "Please close your eyes, Todd." Her voice was soft as the blackness she lived in. She pressed her fingers lightly over his thin lids. She took a deep breath. Todd could not see her so he was unsure of what she was doing, but he began to sense her… that seemed to be the idea here. Sensing things. "Please keep your eyes closed." Her hands slid along his face over the top of his nose to his mouth. She ran her fingertips along the ridge of his upper lip and around to dip across his lower lip. She slowly forced the tips of two of her fingers just slightly into his mouth. He began to breathe more heavily. She seemed not to notice but continued her investigation of his body along his neck and then with two hands circling his ears. "Can you hear the ocean… at night when the tides come in it seems the most powerful element I can experience… I sit here in this room or lie in my bed and feel that I am a part of it… the power of water. Sometimes, when it's warm, I go down at night in a light chemise and walk along the incoming tide. Then, I lie down in the small waves and feel the force of them on my body. "

Todd was being mesmerized as if she was a magician on a stage and he had volunteered. Well, he had volunteered, hadn't he, to be her subject. She was reading him now as certainly as if he was her own book. He began to feel his pulse race. As he had to put his hands somewhere, they had settled on her leg. They were trembling there. He thought to move them along her leg, to read her body as she was reading his. But, he did not. He realized he was illiterate in her language.

Her hands traveled down from his neck to the buttons of his shirt and she undid three of them and pulled his chest bare. "Have you ever noticed that the tips of hair are sensitive… "

Todd shivered under her touch. She seemed a breeze that was warming him. He could not actually feel her fingers, but instead a sensation that covered the whole of his torso... and still further down, he felt arousal. He sensed she had moved her face closer. There was a sweetness of breath close to him.

"This is what it's like to be sightless, Todd. You cannot see people or objects, but you can sense everything... the shift in ocean currents which seem to me to signal a shift in the stars I have never gazed upon... I can see the sun, because I feel it, yet there is no temperature sensation from the moon and I can "see" it. Now here I can cheat and "read" the tide charts and moonrise logs, so I know intellectually that it will be there, so I go out on the deck and gaze at it as if we can communicate, the moon and I. I have more friends than you might imagine... Raleigh, the sun, the tides, the flowers around my tiny house, the moon, my music — Chopin is my complete favorite — and I have yet to speak of the gulls that come to visit."

By now she had taken off Todd's shirt and was undoing his belt. "Like the tides and the stars, I am acting on instinct now. I have never done this, and my sense is that you have never done this either. But, I like the sound of your voice mixed with my Chopin. You have brought me gifts, so now I would like to give you a gift as well. I hope you won't think of me as taking liberties... "

Todd could hardly feel her hands now. His mind kept trying to identify the "second" gift. He had helped her, if there was to be counting, that would be one, but what was the second one. His mind reached for it, but he was sighted and not used to seeing in the dark. He could not find it... though it occurred to him that if he was as sensitive as she, he might be experiencing it now... this moment, under her blind fingers.

She had pulled the belt off its loops, he knew in his heightened awareness, because he heard it slip onto the floor. His fullest sense now was her voice. He had never been hypnotized, but this was what he imagined it to be... her voice slid into his ears, down to his heart and by known pathways, back into his brain where soft-ness lived. Where it was as black as the vision of her eyes. It was though her voice was a silver thread and its silky end could find its way into the deepest part of him.

"… but as you gazed upon my body…" he heard her say, "you called it 'golden', — why then I claim now my right to see the riches of your body. After all, Todd, fair is fair isn't that so… ?

…what is sight for the goose is sense for the gander…"

His erection was full now and though he could not see any of this, he felt it must be raising to the ceiling of this small house, as if perhaps, it could extend itself outside and into the sunlight. He knew she was not touching him there, but that she was circling his orb with the tips of her fingers only the distance of thread away from his skin. Her breath on his face, soft and sweet, lulled his eyes and caressed his lips, as a tender kiss.

He would be blind if this was the way he could feel. He would learn the Braille necessary to penetrate without touch or taste into her being. He would… Todd felt an explosion. Sound was not af-fected by sight, yet it caused a flashing behind his eyes, as though light was attempting to make its way either into or out of his head. Interior illumination. Then a sense of falling as if he had been her leg on the deck and the surface disappeared under him.

Then, silence and true blackness.

When Todd awoke, all was as she had left it… he was sprawled on the sofa, his shirt was off and his belt on the floor beside him. His pants were undone and the coffee cup was half full, but un-touched in front of him beside the partially eaten cinnamon cake. The sun was lower in the sky now, though he could not see it — he could only feel it on his back through the open doors.

He sat up and looked for her. He called for the dog — Raleigh! He stood and put on his clothes, and only then noticed the white piece of notepaper she must have left in his hand.

Dear Todd,

 I hope you have enjoyed your lesson in Braille. You are a good student and a quick learner. I have enjoyed "seeing" your body... as you seem to have enjoyed mine. It was a unique sensibility.
Thank you...

(The end of Kellnur's story, *Braille*)

A Cat in a Man Suit

George Furner led a circumscribed life. He got up at six, fed the cats in the nude, made himself coffee, retrieved the paper from the front porch and sat in the living room, still in the nude, and read the paper from cover to cover. He even read the obituaries.

George had never done that before his favorite cat, Spud — who had been one hundred forty-seven years old — died last March. Spud was a brownish tortoise-shell cat who had talked to George in a squeaky mew and kept him company in the mornings while he shaved. The cat had looked at him deeply at these times.

It was Spudy who had made George understand that he wanted to be a cat, too. As far back as he could remember, George admired the manner in which cats moved, the way they looked directly at a person. There was pleasure in their fur. When George picked up one of his cats and buried his face in it, he knew that a cat didn't smell like anything else. It smelled like cat — as odd as it felt, he wished that he, too, had fur.

When Spud began to fail, George took him to the vet.

"I'm sorry, Mr. Furner," the vet had said softly, "but your cat here is just worn out."

George nodded at the man.

"How old did you say he was?"

"One hundred and forty-seven."

"Oh yes, uh, that's right. 21 years old. Lucky cat."

George had held the cat in his arms and talked to him, but Spudy was too tired even to talk back, though George heard a barely discernible purr. George had done everything to be at the animal hospital when Spud died. The doctor did everything possible to ease the cat's passing. But, when the actuality of that hit George, he was inconsolable.

At the market that night, George bumped into an old friend who worked for the *Canton News*. He blurted out the whole story of the cat's life and his age, which George always referred to in cat years — seven to one. The newspaper friend had never heard of a cat living to age twenty-one, so he convinced his editor to run the cat's obituary in the paper. The reporter called George and told him to look on Page 18B.

By 7:45 on most mornings, George was shaved, dressed, had his bed made, flowers watered and coffee in a thermos ready for the twenty minute drive to the office where he was an insurance adjuster. The only thing that had unbalanced his twenty-three years at this job was Martha's leaving.

"Away," she had said, "I'm going away, George. Far enough away to find someone who'll talk to me more than he talks to his cats." And with that, the union between them blew away like pollen in the spring.

A person couldn't move much farther away from Canton, Ohio, than Fairbanks, Alaska. Martha wrote him often of her new life on the "frontier." He laughed the day he got a letter that included a picture of her and "her" dog. He had known for a while she had been living with a man. He assumed the dog came with the arrangement. George stared at the picture for a long time before he pasted it to the cupboard door that held the cat food.

George could be home most days by 4:45. On a bright summer day, he could be in the garden by five after five — unless the mail for the day was good. Then the garden came later while he had a Schlitz on the wooden bench by his potting shed and went through his small stack of letters.

Today brought a card from Danny. His son always sent him postcards when he traveled. Danny was a lucky traveler, as the door to the potting shed attested. His postcards were tacked to the door three deep. When Danny had come home with his wife for a visit, he had taken a picture of his father standing next to the door. Linda had taken a shot of Danny and George standing together beside the potting shed door so that Danny could show his friends what his father had made for them.

But this card would not go on the door. It would have to go somewhere more special. It was a photograph of a cat. The cat was splotched black and white, with a small triangular shape of black on his nose, a furry face only a mother cat could love. The way the picture had been taken, the cat seemed to be leaning in a cocky way against a wicker stool. A sentence was written over the cat on the postcard: A MAN IN A CAT SUIT.

A man in a cat suit. George mused over that in his head as he worked in the garden in the late afternoon light. This was his night to bowl with the office team. He would have to shower and put on his bowling outfit. All the players wore the same white shirt with All State Tigers stitched on the back. Beneath that, in black letters, was also stitched Canton, O. As he looked at himself in Martha's full length mirror, he wished he did not have to go to bowling tonight. But he went anyway.

When he returned, the cats were all mewing around impatiently, waiting to be fed. He had lost count of how many there were. When he and Martha had been together, there had been four cats, often with a fifth "passing through," as he would say to the kids. Now, that number had edged past fifteen or sixteen. The people who worked at the Supermarket where George shopped made jokes about him. When the store manager noticed how steeply

his buying habits changed, George was offered a by-the-case dis-
count on cat food.

Night-after-Bowling brought a special treat, and many of the
cats followed him around in his bowling outfit until he brought out
the large box of catnip. He rubbed the weed into an oversized
fabric ball in the rec room at the back of the house.

Watching them was as good as a circus. On most bowling
nights, he would watch them tumble with each other and the ball,
then go to bed with their wildcat gyrations spinning in his head. But
as he watched them now, George thought of the card from Danny
and went to the kitchen to get it.

He had already had too many beers at the bowling alley, but he
opened another and went back to the rec room to sit with the cats
and read his postcard again:

Dear Dad,
It's a quickie trip to Portland this week for the sales
meeting. I saw this card and knew it was you. Well, if
the suit fits, put it on. Ha-ha.
Miss you,
DAN

"If the suit fits, put it on." He watched the cats bounce off the
ball, jumping and twisting in the air, pouncing and leaping on each
other. Coiled springs that could balance themselves on the edge
of a wish. The catnip might make them drunk, yet it rarely affected
that fine sense of demeanor, of decorum, of pride in every-hair-in-
place.

I would make a fine cat, George thought. I am an orderly being
who could look a friend in the eye, yet be aloof enough, affection-
ate enough to pick my company. To be a friend, yet not overdo it.

Sitting there, watching the cat show, George had the bubble of fantasy that he could go now, this minute, to the costume store over by the high school, find his way inside and locate a cat costume. He surely wouldn't want to risk putting it on there in the store, because he didn't want to leave his own clothes behind. There might also be the danger of attracting unwanted attention at the wheel of his car wearing a cat suit. He could imagine the look on Danny's face when he heard that his father, dressed in a cat costume, had been pulled over by the night patrol car. No. He should bring the outfit home in a box and change there.

When he pulled into his driveway, he noticed the light on in Lorna Miller's house across the street. She must never sleep, he thought. He wondered if she watched him from behind curtains. In the house, he went upstairs with the box containing his suit. He didn't want the cats to see him change. Before he did, he sprinkled extra catnip on the floor in the rec room and on the play-ball they loved. Then, the revel moved on padded feet toward ecstasy. Yet, some of the less energetic had slipped off to the side of the room for rest or washing. One, Sadie, sat right on the floor heater in the middle of summer and began to doze.

The Brothers Four, identical marmalade cats, posed themselves in mirror image on the clawed sofa to watch the continuing carnival, lead now by Sugar, the biggest druggie of them all.

Sugar, with a strong whiff of catnip, started at one corner of the room, racing toward the ball, grazed it doing sixteen miles per hour, and walked around the opposite corner two feet off the floor. It was as Sugar was making her twenty-third lap across the room that the new cat paused in the doorway and surveyed the room. Sugar stopped, not quite in midair, paused to look, and then walked over to inspect the newcomer.

Two or three others continued to roll on the rug over weed spilled off the ball, seemingly unconcerned. Pancho and Whisk, however, moved to a spot halfway between the ball and the doorway. They sat busying themselves with a ruffled place in their fur while Sugar sniffed the stranger up and over. Then, they moved to him, circling, whiffing. It was as if they were the Welcome Wagon ladies. Once they had given their sniff of approval, well, it was a catnip free-for-all.

The newcomer padded along with Whisk toward the ball to join in the madcap frenzy. But first he had to do something he had always wanted to do. He left Whisk and Pancho to move among all the cats, brushing against them. Sniffing as well as being sniffed. Looking directly into eyes. Not to be rude about it, not too close to be offensive, but to have that sense of fur. What an exquisite world this was. How elegant and controlled, yet there was Sugar, grace to the wind, having her fling. To the new cat, this seemed a perfect balance of every aspect of the senses on the point of a pin. It was only then, in the midst of this reflection, that he caught a whiff of the catnip, and understood the deeper meaning of the many lives of a cat.

One part of the animals jumped into a velvet box, safely out of harm's way; the other part abandoned everything to an odor to be floated upon, lost to, joined with. Oh, Lord of Cats, catch me!

The new cat found himself rolling wildly on the floor with Pancho and Whisk, as if to make a cape of the wondrous catnip. The object seemed to be to get as much of the stuff as possible caught up in your fur, lick some off, and then leap some off as you jumped straight up to catch the rays of the ceiling light, no mere moon. The elegant part was the abandonment with the others, claws sheathed, batting, battling as if the jungle was everywhere, hiding them from the seeing world. Finally, he, Pancho and Whisk joined together in a game of chasing tails. They interlaced each other, constantly moving, tails flicking furiously this way and that, paws countering, fainting, circling — until, on one pass, each hit a tail at once, and they all rolled over on the floor in a pile of cat, a ball of paws.

The new cat now found himself facing the fabric ball. He began milking it with his paws as he had done with his mother when he was a kitten. This was better, even, than the catnip. It seemed that he did it for hours, days. As he rolled away from the ball, his forehead flat on the floor, looking upside down at his companions, all had come to quiet. Most now were napping. A few, like Sugar, were washing away the weed, back to every hair in place.

He pulled himself up and with one bound was atop the ball, sitting there, looking over the litter of cats. This was his kingdom, and he their new Prince. He thought of his friend Spud. If only Spudy had lived to see this. To see him now. He flicked his ears. He knew that if Spud were alive, they would have been friends. That Spud, old as he was, would have rallied and played with him, would have rolled with him, licked his fur, been the older brother to his kitten. And when the frolic was over, the old cat would have turned to him, to stare in his way, as if to say they would always be in it together. They were fur, and that was that. Spud would do then what he always had done, pad off to the corner near the heat, curl up on the rug, eyes over bushy tail, to sleep the sleep of an old cat.

In the morning, Sadie moved away from the floor heater to arrange herself on a wide patch of sunlight. Sugar, Pancho, Whisk and the others were still deep in cat dreams. There came a banging on a door at the front of the house. Ears cocked, all the cats heard it and looked up to see if it would affect them.

No, it seemed not. But it was past time to eat, the new cat thought, why hadn't someone come to feed him and the others. The banging on the front door continued.

Candied Buns, Sugared Breasts

A lusty confectionary

All lovers delight

The body bakery

Is open all night.

The White Feather

They called her the white feather
because
well, she was perfect. Beautiful, bendable
but not breakable.

She flowed the currents following her feather's heart
to unimagined heights on wafting currents
filling the world with brushed freedom and strength.

No man could keep her.
They were weak, even imperfect, ambitious,
and worse, possessive.
A poor match for her rootlessness.

So, she left man after man,
Not in search of perfection,
but for ruthless honesty
and
a certain flexibility.

Nevertheless,
she made it known, when a truly flexible man makes love to her,
she may stay.

Yet…

The Storm

The terrain is so vast I constantly lose myself in it.

I am alert for "landmarks" to keep my bearings.
My natural being keeps searching for
sunlight, for warmth.
Warmth reminds me of home,
yet now I have lost hope of ever finding
my way back.

I meet a wolf. He is beautiful. We travel together.
I admire his sense of place, of distance.
Most of all, his inner compass.

A storm comes. We lose each other.
My first thought is to search for him, but I realize
I should wait.
I find a high place. I build a fire,
a large fire with a hole in the middle.
I walk around the fire as it ignites itself.
Then, I step into the middle.

If I were God looking down at me
I would be an eye looking up at him.
I laugh knowing this to be an illusion.
I am not an eye.
There is no God.
There is no fire.
I am mad.

Then, the wolf returns and stands beside me.
I touch him. His fur is soft.
The storm clears.
We curl together as if the storm had lasted for years.

It was Hanna who insisted that This Story go into *Janet's Annex*. Hanna found it when Jannie took her back to the apartment to look at "the chapter search."

The House in Westchester County

They passed home after home, some larger and imposing, othersjust "nicely done" and many with lovely large gardens. Dennis would neveradmit that he was a bit intimidated, but Martha was enchanted. Living here became more and more "an idea" in her mind.

"How much did you say this property was?" It was Dennis who asked the crucial question.

They were sitting in the back of Mr. Cullen's comfy real estate car. Martha was watching Westchester County pass by with growing envy. She smiled and turned to the rear view mirror to see Mr. Cullen's eyes say, "As it stands, $392,500."

Beside her, Dennis rolled his eyes at no one in general and continued watching the idyl riches roll by.

"How long did you say you folks had been married?" asked Cullen.

Dennis said, "'Bout three, four months."

"Eleven weeks," said Martha. "Eleven weeks next Tuesday."

Cullen nodded, taking in the unspoken ambience between the two. He had been selling property here for, well, eleven years, but he had never had a property like this one, nor clients as potentially odd as these. But, he shrugged inside his body and watched Westchester County roll by. It was a lovely place to live, and it took a certain amount of cash to manage that. And, he couldn't wait to see the response to this house.

"Wow," said Dennis, "what's that place?

"Belongs to the Sucannon's, old family from Upstate who made good in the city. It's part home and part, whatever they are interested in now, and they have pretty wide margins.

Dennis turned to Martha and whispered, "Shouldn't we just give this up? I mean, Martha, look…" He gestured out the window. Martha smiled at him and patted his hand as if to say… but, her attention was immediately pulled away.

"…that looks like a nice place, right there, the Friends' Meeting… a community kind of place — are we getting close?" Martha asked just as Cullen was already slowing down. She pointed out the Meeting place, as the real estate man was allowing her see it more fully, but shortly thereafter, he turned to the left, just across from and past the Friends' Meeting Center to the driveway of the property.

Dennis made a short howling sound. Mr. Cullen caught it in the rear view mirror, as he reached to turn off the ignition of the car. Martha leaned out the window of the car, as if to get closer to the building, as if to immediately intuit it.

"This is the place," said Mr. Cullen, without fanfare.

They were faced with what had been a large white house, lovely in its inception, however many years ago, but now, a dirty white shell of its former past, tattered and lonely… in need of the direst face-lift.

They got out, first Martha in awe. Finally, Dennis pulled himself out of the back seat and stretched his legs, as if to say that it was good to have a brief rest stop before going back to the real estate office.

Martha walked up to the front door as if to intuit something.

Then, she began circling the house and gazing at the outbuildings, mainly the tattered almost falling down garage building. Martha could hear the voice of her Great Aunt Martha, for whom she had been named, whispering — or perhaps standing in the back of her mind. What-was-it-that Auntie M. was saying? Martha looked off to where Dennis and the real estate man were standing, waiting for her. Dennis ready to get back in the car, Mr. Cullen fishing for his key to the house. It was as if, Martha thought, this was some sort of a puzzle or game they were playing.

At the front door, Mr. Cullen rustled more with the keys and finally opened the worn door and Martha stepped right in. Dennis hung back, wondering if his new wife had lost her senses. How, he thought, could anyone be even willing to *walk into such a place*. This gave him pause.

What surprised them all was how clean and tidy the entry way was. It looked swept and mopped and opened right onto the main room downstairs.

"Oh my God," it was Martha. The pull of her surprise drew them into this main room right behind her. She was standing on the carpet turning herself in a circle to see the walls around her, all of which were covered with artwork, lovely framed artwork.

Mr. Cullen gasped. Dennis shook his head, as if he had seen a spook. Martha immediately began circling the room, taking in each piece of artwork as if they has suddenly been transported to the local Museum... no, no, thought Cullen, this was the living room of a well-off couple who got into art for décor — "all right" art for their home, early on. **How could this be?** The last time he had been here, some months ago now, it looked on the inside as a mirror im-age of the outside.

Martha finished circling the room. She turned to Cullen. "I sup-pose you have an explanation for this..." she waved her arm as if to take up the whole room in one sweep, as if she was in one of the well-appointed homes just down the road.

"I... ah, I, well, I really don't. This is impossible."

Dennis spoke up, now suspicious of the whole set-up. "Com'on, Cullen, cut the crap. You are the real estate dealer responsible for this, there is no way in hell you could *not* be aware of this..." and Dennis did a slower take on what Martha had just done around the room.

Martha turned away from them and walked quickly into the adjoining room, the dining area as it turned out. She gasped. Here was a small mural — an assemblage-collage where the central theme seemed to be "maps". Parisian street scenes with a scattering of objects like dice, keys and stamps. It was quite successful, she thought — a classic-style and most becoming. Other walls in this room had smaller, simpler work on them: a drawing of a child, a collage in the spirit of the alphabet, a panel of three photographs of what might be the nearby woods, yet taken in an abstract manner. She turned in a circle, slowly taking in the completeness of the room. What an amaz... and then the rising voices of the men in the next room caught her and shook her for a moment before she could bring herself back to this place, this small amazing room... what to think, what to think...

There was a chair. She sat. This needs some deeper understanding and she realized immediately that the shouting of the men in the next room would not find an explanation for what was happening here — happening here? — Martha re-traced her steps to begin looking at everything she had already seen, only more closely.

She went back into the living room and began to see what had at first glance seemed orderly, was in fact, makeshift. The walls had been carefully painted over or cleaned, there was a carpet on the floor, but the floor itself had not been cleaned or refinished. The windows and sills were still a mess, yet the windows separated artwork that had been carefully and thoughtfully hung as if for a "show" of work by a single artist. A single artist, yes... of course, but...

"Goddamnit, Cullen, why don't you just say what this is, own up to it, instead of insisting that all this is a surprise..." Dennis yelling at the top of his voice at the real estate man as if to torture an explanation out of him by pounding the air around him. Cullen said it thirteen times by now... that... "...do you think I am stupid enough to bring anyone here and ask for 400 grand if I didn't know this property like the back of my hand. I tell you AGAIN, I don't know anything about this..." he almost twirled as he waved his hands at the spinning room.

"Yes." said Dennis

"Yes, what?" said Cullen

"Yes, I can imagine that you could be that stupid. I mean, look at this..." and now Dennis mimicked Cullen's wave-around, turn-around.

Halfway through this craziness, Martha had turned away from the men to continue her "tour" or was it an "examination" of the place... moving now to the upstairs.

The rooms upstairs had "drop carpeting" like downstairs with cleaned or painted walls and more artwork, but separated into a gaggle of rooms as if a string of mini-galleries, each with its own theme.

The master bedroom had a series of photographs where each wall might be a separate phase of an artist's life: a wall of simple scenics, a wall of light abstracts in mixed color and black and white. On the other hand, on a wall where the bed might go was a series of nude bodies of a man and a woman in fabric tunnels — as if they were trying to be with each other but the gravity and the fabric made it difficult to touch each other — yet more interesting to watch as a series of images. Martha was particularly taken with these, so sensuous, so full of yearning.

The final wall in this room was a spread of small boxes with assemblages of seemingly random objects collected together — again and again in the whole of this place, there was the sense of trying to "be together" of reaching and searching and finding or never finding. She found it hard to explain to herself, yet she *knew* it was about feeling… yearning.

Martha was stunned. She had been in three rooms upstairs, each had different yet stunning artwork, but no paintings or sculpture, yet many "themes". Here was an artist, a man, she assumed, who was obsessed with obsession and odds and ends, keys and maps, yet at the same time, doing a body of work that is professional and provocative. *Who* is this person, more important, *where* is this person?

The last thought that came to Martha was that she would like, more than anything, to *meet* the person who had done this. What kind of man could this be?

"Martha… Martha… where are you?" It was Dennis, she could hear him coming up the steps with a second pair of footsteps behind him, the real estate man. This broke the bubble of her thoughts, an intrusion, she thought. She had not realized she had been so deeply drawn into this — whatever "this" was. Might be a good idea, said someone in the back of her mind, to pay attention to this.

Dennis walked into the room, waving his arms, "com'on, Darlin', we're leaving **this mess**. Mr. Cullen here," he turned to see Cullen right behind him, "…says he doesn't have a clue 'bout how all this stuff," here Dennis waved his arms around the room they were standing in — one he himself had not looked at… "…got to be here. And clearly, this whole place is wacko enough to run away from, so let's go find ourselves another real estate company."

"Martha," it was Cullen speaking quietly now, "I am most sorry and embarrassed about this. As I tried to explain to your husband, Dennis, I mean, that all this…" he gestured to the new artwork in this room that neither he nor Dennis have looked at, "is a mystery and a surprise to me. I have not shown this property in some time for many obvious reasons, but, you," here he referred directly to Martha, "you seem to be a bit more adventurous than the regular home buyer, so , I thought…" he shrugged, "that because of the location and the very land value, you might want to see another idea. I mean…"

Dennis interrupted,"Listen, Darlin', there is no point to this and I am getting very hungry and very, very tired of listening to Mr. Cullen here, play us along…"

"I think there is a point to this." Martha whispered.

Dennis looked sternly at her, "What do you mean?"

"Have you looked around here?" she said.

"No, 'course not," said Dennis. "This is a very high class, low class, mysterious piece of… ah property. If I were him," Dennis jerked his thumb at Cullen, "I would ask the owner of this piece of, well, this place, to level it and try to sell it to some folks who were best friends with a contractor."

Martha's tone softened. "Dennis, just take a look here. I mean, take a look. The inside of this house has been lovingly what… arranged by an intelligence that is trying to either do something, or make a point, or express something that is difficult-by-far to say, or show or tell. Think about that person for a moment, Dennis… what must a person who can form or gather or create something like this — what must a person be like who can create walls like this?" and here Martha turned herself around to all the walls before facing Dennis.

"Right you are, Darlin'… he's crazy, craz…" Dennis let that sink in. He turned to Cullen as if to ask a question, but changed his mind. He walked up to his wife and put his arms around her, "Listen, Sweetheart," he whispered in Martha's ear, "you have asked a question that none of us guys, " he pointed to Cullen, "have been smart enough to ask: What kind of a lunatic would put all this stuff on the walls and then leave — and by the way, where did he get all this stuff?" It was the way Dennis said "stuff" that ruffled Martha.

"If it was a man, and I think it was, who created this 'stuff', he is an Artist and an interesting one. I would like to meet him, and know more about his artwork."

"You can't be serious."

"I am most serious."

Martha and Dennis turned to Cullen for an answer. Cullen looked from one to the other and then a turn-a-round of the walls. Cullen finally just raised his hands, as if one of the couple had pointed a gun at him. There was a deep sense in him not only not to speak, but not to interfere with this "family discussion." He had known plenty of prospective clients like Dennis, but not one like Martha — she was different, very, very different. Cullen nodded to her, as if to urge her to continue her thoughts.

"Dennis, honey, would you do me a small favor? Would you walk around the walls in these rooms and look at the artwork that has been hung here by someone. I would like to know, not what you think the motives were of the person — but what of the care of the hanging of these rooms like art galleries and then, the artwork itself. What do you think of that — the   art   work?"

Dennis looked at her as if she had asked him to put on some lipstick. "Why, Darlin'? Why do I need to do that, we are not buying this house, with or without all this stuff…" more waving of arms— "on the walls."

Dennis paused to look at Martha.

Martha took the opportunity to look at Dennis.

Cullen held his breath.

"We are tryin', Darlin', listen to me, we are tryin' to buy a house and get settled. We don't like this house, we don't like or trust this guy…" here he pushed his arms toward Cullen. "…who is trying to sell us this, ah, this place. Actually, he is not trying to sell it to us anymore, because he doesn't even understand his own property any more — so, we are out of here…" Dennis stood aside for Martha to leave first.

Martha felt a movement behind her, or perhaps within her, she wasn't certain. She didn't look around to be certain, she only looked at her new husband, Dennis Stockbridge. The fellow she had been married to for eleven weeks, going on twelve. Martha felt she was in a strange country, but suddenly she had emerged from dense woods to see a river, a clear river and a way across this river to the other side. It was a bridge, all her life she had loved bridges. Her father had sensed that in her and built for her a small bridge across the small pond behind their house — one that Martha could walk across at any time, in any season, on any whim. The bridge she was now facing in this room felt like the mighty Golden Gate Bridge across a vast, ah, pond. This was a new kind of bridge she faced.

She looked from Dennis to Cullen and the distance between them. "I want to buy this house, Mr. Cullen. I believe you said the price was $392,500. I don't feel any need to haggle with you, you had said 'as is', so I'll take it 'as is'."

Before Dennis could say anything, and he was bursting, Cullen said, "Well, I'm sorry Martha, but I won't be able to sell it to you until I speak with my superiors back at the office, and the owner about… ah… all this…" a waving of arms toward the walls.

"Yes, you will, Mr. Cullen. You will drive me to your offices and fill out your voluminous paperwork and I will write you a check for the amount of the sale."

"…a check…" said Cullen.

"…cash!" she said.

"Whaaaaaa…" said Dennis, '"…wait the hell a minute here, Darlin', I got a say in this and it's one word…"

"I hope it's yes, Dennis, I really do hope for "yes". You see, Dennis, Mr. Cullen is caught between the devil and a hard place. I am offering him cash for this, he thinks, hopeless property that has been on the market since whoever was President, and now, he can unload it, 'cause if he doesn't, and we tell the owner that Mr. Cullen has balked — no need to mention the surprising inner 'décor' — Mr. Cullen will be out in the cold, or freelancing, or worse…"

"…but, Darlin', I don't want to live here. I know that means something to you."

Martha walked up to Dennis and again put her arms fully around him and said, "Yes, it does mean something to me, I had hoped you would give in to this whim of mine…" she tightened her arms around him, "…and say you would be happy to take a flyer with me on this place. We could fix it up, the location and the neighborhood are, well, probably priceless, the house needs, yes, some fixing up, but we can do that and then we will love it. After all, who can buy a house nowadays that is completely decorated with original artwork on walls that have been recently painted." At "recently painted" both men turned to look at the walls behind the artwork. Yes, it had been painted…

"Dennis, I want to live here and I want to live here with you, no matter what you think of the artwork — we *are* talking about US."

Before Dennis could think of a response, everyone in the room, heard Dennis say, "No." Martha shook slightly and nodded, first at Dennis, then at Cullen. "Well, if nothing else, he is direct."

She turned to look behind her, then back at Dennis. "My Great Aunt Martha left me enough money to get my married life started. It was in her will: When my lovely Martha marrys, I hope it will be happy and productive and I wish her to begin that new life with a house she loves and is her own. These monies will provide that."

Martha looked at Cullen. "My Aunt Martha was a good and smart and wise and thrifty woman. There are quite enough monies to buy this house and it's in the bank, and…" she reached inside her purse and shook a check book at both the men. "I have my check book with me. I want to buy this house. I want to buy it to-day."

She walked up to Dennis and hugged him hard, and kissed him deeply and whispered, "Goodbye, Dennis, don't forget that I love you."

Martha walked down the stairs, leaving the men above their own feelings. She stood in the middle of the living room and said to herself...

"I know he will come... I just know it..."

Lightning Source UK Ltd.
Milton Keynes UK
UKOW03f1515300117
293183UK00002B/546/P